7.95

EDUCATION
LIBRARY

QUEEN'S UNIVERSITY
AT KINGSTON

KINGSTON ONTARIO CANADA

D1156788

Carry My Bones Northwest

By the Same Author

ON THE TRAIL OF LONG TOM
MESSAGE FROM ARKMAE
SEVEN FOR THE SEA

Carry My Bones Northwest

W. TOWRIE CUTT

ANDRE DEUTSCH

Juv.
PS8555.U87C37

First published 1973 by
André Deutsch Limited
105 Great Russell Street London wc1

Copyright © 1973 by W. Towrie Cutt
All rights reserved

Printed in Great Britain by
Cox & Wyman Ltd
London, Fakenham and Reading

isbn 0 233 96478 9

CONTENTS

To DODDY,
the one remaining brother

I

June 24th, 1794

In the early morning, two boys, about five and six, played by the little prairie stream that flowed swiftly to the near-by Pigogomew, the south branch of the Saskatchewan. They had fashioned rough little canoes out of a piece of birch bark found in the copse on the bank, and had just launched them. They watched as their two boats whirled round the sunlit bend and disappeared from sight.

'We'll find them at the fort, Ayek,' shrilled the smaller boy, hitching up his buckskin trousers which had slipped down in the launching.

'No, they sink in the rough water in the river, Willie,' answered Ayek, his dark eyes on the stream. His naked body above his trousers was a darker shade of brown than Willie's.

'Willie!' came a voice from the copse above them.

'Indians come to trade,' muttered Ayek as he and Willie went up the grassy bank with its dying blue crocuses, and its tiny buttercups over which small butterflies of forget-me-not blue fluttered. On the grass sat a tall man clad in a red shirt and buckskin trousers, and beside him sat a woman, her deerskin leggings heavily beaded, her leather skirt embroidered at the hem, and wearing a dyed porcupine-quill necklace above her cotton blouse. The man was William Fea, a labourer for the Hudson's Bay Company, the woman, Ekkowloh, his Indian wife. The two boys stood straight and silent before the man.

'Willie, we're sending you home to your grandfather over the sea,' said the man. 'When my time's out, your mother and I will come.'

Willie looked blankly at his father. Ayek looked and questioned.

'Home? My grandfather home in the tent at the fort. My father gone to Hudson's Bay with furs. Willie's grandfather down there?'

'No, Ayek. Away across the sea, two moons from Hudson's Bay. Willie will go in a ship.'

'Ship – the big boat that brings out the axes and saws and guns. The sea, that is a big lake.'

'It is salt, and big, yes; a lake that would reach from here to the mountains and down to the bay.'

'Mountains are a moon from here, and the bay a moon.'

Willie was only half listening while looking at his mother, who looked back at her son, her black eyes sad. He turned to his father.

'You send me away,' he whispered.

'Yes, Willie. You will learn to read and write, and become a trader like Jamie Tait, and come back to be a master at the fort,' answered his father, remembering how friendly the boy had been with James Tait who had gone from the fort a month earlier.

Willie's eyes dropped. He shuffled over to his mother and let out a stifled sob.

'Brave never make sound, Willie,' admonished Ayek.

Ekkowloh spoke bitterly. 'Chief Tomison say Willie will go. We go here, we go there, when Chief Tomison says go. We do not choose.' She fondled the boy's arm, but he pulled away and turned from the group.

His father spoke gently. 'Mr Tomison will try to arrange a passage at the Bay for you, Willie. But you will not go to your grandfather across the sea until summer has gone and winter has gone. He may not be able to get you a passage. Then you would stay here and be a trapper and a canoe man, and freeze and starve in winter. And you would have to go to the Indian wars. Mr Tomison is good.'

'Come,' said Ekkowloh, 'we go back to the fort.'

Ayek started out, and Willie followed slowly. Ayek turned and hurried him forward. 'You go, Willie. I stay. My father come back. He go on warpath with gun. Meet Gros Ventres. Bang! Bang! Gros Ventres have no guns. I go when I am a brave. You come back big white chief, and bring me gun.'

Willie did not answer. His eyes were on the ground; his moccasins dragged in the fresh prairie grass. Behind him his father walked thoughtfully. The boy would understand some day. Mr Tomison had offered a gift that could not be refused. Ekkowlow was also thoughtful. Her boy, so young, was to go from her. She accepted the sad fact with the fatalism of an Indian mother whose lot was to bear burdens. Her son would come back a master, and she, now better fed and clothed than other Indian wives, would be provided for in her old age, if, as William feared, his father would not have her in his home across the sea. James Tait was to visit the old man when he got across the water, and try to convince him that an Indian could make a good wife and mother, even though she was a heathen.

The four came to the river where their canoe was beached opposite the fort. South Branch House stood on the high bank of the Pigogomew, and was protected by a stockade, with one gate facing the river and another facing the prairie behind the fort. Inside the stockade were the storehouse, the quarters for the four men servants of the Hudson's Bay, and a dozen Indian tents which sheltered a dozen Indian women (wives of the Indians who were away in canoes taking the winter's furs down to the bay), their children and their aged parents. Magnus Annal, the man in charge, had come to the fort a month earlier, relieving James Tait whose time with the Company was up. Tomison, the inland master of all the forts, had brought Annal from the upper Saskatchewan, when the furs were taken away, and had taken Tait back with him. Tomison would go to Britain in the same ship as Tait, as he had been recalled to London to give the directors information.

Willie had brightened up on reaching the river. He and Ayek hurried into the canoe and seized the paddles.

'We can paddle it right across, Father,' he said.

William Fea allowed them to try. In the strong central current Willie strove his hardest to match Ayek, and did so. A glow lighted his face as they came into shallow water, and his father said, 'Well paddled, Willie. You two boys take the old canoe and keep out of the midstream.'

'You're a good canoe man, Willie,' said his mother, as Willie and Ayek hurried off to the old canoe, Willie either having forgotten that he might have to leave the fort and Ayek, or having accepted it fatalistically as his mother's people did.

The boys sent the old canoe downstream, both paddling furiously, and then Ayek back paddled, whirling the canoe around. They struggled against the current, not very strong near the river flat, glancing up at the bank where Willie's father joined the other two men seated there. Opposite them, the boys back paddled, and Ayek with his greater strength, sent the canoe outwards. A shout came from the bank.

'What he telling us?' questioned Ayek.

'He says keep away from the deep water. And we paddled the other canoe over it!'

'This canoe old, Willie. There Magnus Annal, come looking for Indians.'

'Aye, he wants furs and dried meat. Jamie Tait traded much with Indians and Mr Tomison won't be pleased if Magnus gets little.'

'They all go to back gate, Willie. We go too.'

The boys hauled their canoe half out of the water, placed the paddles on the beach, and went up the slope to the fort. By the open gate, Jon Van Driel sat smoking.

'Welcome to South Branch House, Indian braves,' he said jocularly. 'Have you furs for their Honours of the Hudson's Bay Company?'

'No, we go seek furs through back gate,' answered Ayek. 'You come, Jon?'

'I must watch the river,' the man answered shortly, 'for what never comes.'

'We go look back gate,' answered Ayek, and the two boys went into the fort. They passed the cabins and store-house, and the close-pitched tents of the Indian women and old men, all the young men being away to the Bay. The boys hurried to catch the three men, now joined by Watchusk the Indian interpreter, who would speak with any Indians who might chance along, and bring furs to trade.

The men walked slowly, and the two boys, practising the warpath, stalked one another in the long green grass.

Each would almost disappear and lie as still as a rock, watching for the slightest movement from the other. Then they began to crawl up on the men as if they were the foe. Just as Ayek got to the heels of the Interpreter, Watchusk stopped, shading his eyes as he looked south into the sun.

'Indian come,' he said gutturally.

'Grand! We'll get them before the pedlars,' cried Annal, as he hurried on with the other two men.

Little Willie now stood by Watchusk and Ayek, and saw in the distance mounted Indians quite unlike the Pigogomews or any Cree. Suddenly Watchusk shouted: 'Gros Ventres. Run!'

Hugh Brough turned back laughing. 'Oh, come on, Watchusk. All Indians are friends to Hudson's Bay men.'

'Not to Cree. Enemy of Cree. Gros Ventres, on warpath. Run. Run to fort, cubs,' he hissed to the boys.

Watchusk turned and ran. Ayek ran. Little Willie stood looking from his father to the approaching riders, on horses of roan, piebald, and iron-grey, and then at their faces hideously painted in red, yellow and black. He ran towards his father on whom the spread-out Indians were now closing in. Too late, the three men turned, Willie Fea running to his son. The Indians leapt from their horses, brandishing knives and tomahawks, and shouted their terrible war cries.

'Run, Willie, run,' cried his father, as an Indian struck him down.

Little Willie, his limbs shaking, stood still as an Indian waved aloft a bloody thing, his father's scalp. The boy fell in the long grass in a dead faint.

The bitter smell of smoke brought him to consciousness.

As he raised his body with his arms, a pounding shook the plain, and horses' hooves thudded towards him. He rolled over on his face, and lay stiff. The dull thuds of galloping feet sounded in his ears as if they were coming full upon him. On they thudded. Then all was quiet.

A dense cloud of smoke rolled over him as he lay fearful and stiff. It came and went, rose and fell, acrid and suffocating. At last it cleared, and the boy raised himself to look into the sinking sun towards the fort. Four oblongs of fallen logs puffed fitfully. All the tents were gone; not a living creature stirred. He rose slowly upright, and gazed around. The land was empty. Only the puffs from these four oblongs stirred. One small boy stood in a vast wilderness.

He looked down at the bedded patch his body had made in the grass, for he could not bring himself to look to the place where his father, Hugh Brough, and Magnus Annal lay. He moved slowly towards the fort, lifting one leg and then the other. Suddenly he stopped, rigid and horror-struck. There lay the body of Ayek, face down, the back of his head all bloody. When little Willie was able to breathe again, he went slowly round the spot where his playmate lay, his dark eyes averted. At last he approached the gate, and stopped again with a jerk. Watchusk lay prone on the grass just to one side of the gate.

Crammed full of horror, the boy went on listlessly through the gate, to see mangled corpses litter the enclosure. In between slashed and fallen tents he passed bodies of women, of children, and of old men. No longer able to feel, he expected only to see more blood-drenched forms lying hunched on the ground. He turned from the fallen tents to the smoking logs, and as he did so, caught sight of his mother, her head and neck clotted in dark red, her buckskin skirt bunched over the backs of her knees. He could not go near, but ran down the bank to the river.

A short distance downstream an old canoe was drawn up, the same that Ayek and he had hauled up that morning. The boy dashed for it, and tried to push it into the water. He strove and strained, his bare feet sinking in the mud. Out of breath, he straightened up, looking towards the smoking ruins. There was a movement, very slight, just to one side of the remains of the storehouse, near the old cellar into which rubbish had been flung.

A head emerged, no hat, the fair hair full of dirt and sawdust. Then the shoulders. Willie shrank down by the canoe. The head turned in jerks, downstream, upstream, and to the smoking ruins. The boy did not move; he noted that the fair hair was not red-stained, nor were the shavings that clung to the hair. The head again rotated slowly, and a form emerged. Willie saw it was Jon Van Driel. After a last glance around, the man came racing to the very spot where Willie crouched.

The boy rose. The man stiffened in his tracks, shavings trembling on the stiff hairs, wild eyes rolling in a blackened face, and stared at the tiny figure for some time.

'Oh! Little Willie!' he croaked in relief. 'Take the paddles, boy. Haste.'

Willie grabbed the paddles and scrambled into the canoe. Van Driel pushed it into the river with such force that he fell into the shallow water, pulling the craft down with a thud. He recovered, lumbered dripping aboard, seized a paddle from the boy, and drove the canoe into the current.

The boy lay weak in the stern. The man, paddling with frenzy, sent the canoe racing down the strong June current. His breathing sounded heavier and heavier as they shot along. He stopped momently to turn his head and roll his eyes first to one bank and then to the other, while gasps escaped him as if his lungs would burst. Still he kept on, great beads of sweat rolling from his blackened forehead, around his wild eyes, to streak his smoke-stained face. At last he gave a groan and slumped exhausted into the bottom of the canoe, his paddle striking Willie on the arm.

The canoe turned broadside to the stream, a rapid was ahead, and the boy feared they would be swamped. The paddle the man had dropped was far behind. Willie, realising that he held the other paddle in his hand, dipped it over and stroked, straightening the canoe to the current, and sending it rushing through the rapid. Willie gently stroked to keep it straight while it raced over the white waters, and kept it in the current when the cataract was passed. Then, while the current crossed from high bank to low bank, he looked fearfully over his shoulder. Not a sign of a Gros Ventre or of any other human being.

On went the canoe while the sun sank and the wind died down, and the twilight grew dim. Small birds skimmed past, picking up insects. A fish plunged, startling the little boy who was wondering if the man were dead. He lay still, his body bent, one arm upflung over his black face. Willie heard a long-drawn sigh, then another, and the man lay still again.

Willie hoped that Van Driel would not die. He himself kept on stroking lightly, but a great weariness crept over him so that he paddled automatically. Night hawks whirred over the land. The light died away leaving a mere luminosity on the waters, the wooded banks being dark and ominous. Willie's eyelids closed; he forced them open. They closed again.

When he awoke, the sun was high in the sky. Van Driel was paddling steadily, not in jerks. The river was now very wide, the current swift. When Van Driel turned to see the boy awake, red streaks still showed in a face not quite so black.

'You lost a paddle, Little Willie,' he said gently.

'You let one go in the water,' mumbled Willie. 'I paddled with mine.'

'Little boy, you saved us both. We're far past the junction, and might be in Cumberland tonight.'

He turned his streaked face forward, and bent to his work, paddling steadily. On they went, hour after hour. The man handed Willie the paddle while he rested, but only for a few moments, always paddling faster for a time after the boy returned the paddle to him.

On they swept with the swift stream, past gravel bars and islets, the sun swinging round behind them. Hour after hour, man and boy near exhaustion, while the long summer day ended with the sinking of the sun. But darkness did not fall, even when Van Driel turned into Cumberland at midnight. Beyond the dark confines of shore and the reflections framing a still glittering surface, men stood on a landing wondering what the slow-approaching canoe could hold.

Shortly, one of them lifted an unconscious boy from the canoe, and carried him up, while two others supported Van Driel to Cumberland House. Soon the men were listening horrified as the man incoherently told of the destruction of South Branch House and all its inmates except little Willie Fea and himself.

2

Ardvik, Orkney - 1794

James Tait paced steadily down the slope of the long-rolling Orkney hill in the late sunshine of an October day. He wondered how the Feas would take the message which his friend, William Fea, had asked him to give when he had talked with him at South Branch House in the warm sunshine of early summer. Not only was William sending his half-breed son, Little Willie, to his parents, but also he intended to bring his Indian wife home with him when he came in two years' time. It might help that three men had already brought Indian wives who were excellent workers home to Orkney, but Tait doubted it. Old William Fea was well-known for his strong disapproval of what he called 'heathen marriages', and anyway the women of the islands had always worked from morning to night, in the house, in the fields, and in the byres and barns. Tomison, the inland master for all the Hudson's Bay posts, had said he would communicate with the Feas and make William's way smooth. Yet, as much as Tomison's word would help, it did not make Tait's job easy. He had promised, however, and he must do it.

Tait mused on Tomison's interest in the boy, Little Willie Fea. When the baby was born, Tomison had insisted that Fea take the mother to wife, and gossip round the posts had it that he was really Tomison's son. Tait, knowing how strict the master was and how deep was his interest in schooling, did not believe the gossip. Far more likely Tomison saw in the lad a future master for the Hudson's Bay Company, one with the advantages of Indian blood and instinct, like Moses Norton, governor at Fort Prince of Wales.

As Tait mused on other things he had heard of Walter Fea, the task he had undertaken seemed even harder. He was said to be a successful and ambitious farmer, renting a farm for seventy pounds a year from the laird, and he no doubt thought of his son returning with quite a bit of money, and making an advantageous marriage with some prosperous farmer's or laird's daughter. Mrs Fea, however, was said to be a kindly soul.

Tait rested for a while, looking down at the scattered houses along the bay called Ardvik. The slightly ruffled waters stretched out green and purple to the blue of the strong-flowing strait that swept between Hrossey and Hrolfsey. From the foot of a long, brown hill the land lay in green and yellow patches on either side of the inlet, and beyond green islands, large and small, separated by firths and sounds lay to the north as far as eye could see. The treeless land bore little resemblance to the land round South Branch House unless one imagined the sea as the plain and the islands as the woods and copses that marked the west where the prairie ended and the Great Northern Forest began.

Eight little houses a few hundred yards apart were scattered along a rough road that skirted the bay and cut across the two headlands on either side. Their roofs showed yellow in the sunlight, five with weeds growing in the old thatch, three with new-thatched roofs. Both to the south and to the north lay larger houses, slate-roofed, their windows glittering in the sunshine. Between the larger houses and the cottages were two medium-sized farms, houses and steadings with flagstone roofs. Since Tait had first left Orkney the run-rig system (by which the owners rented small patches separated by ridges to cottars) had given place to the larger farm rented to good farmers like Walter Fea, leaving only the poorer land to the cottars.

Although Tait had come prepared to soften up the Feas for his news, his inside pocket bulging with a bottle of whisky, he feared that a quiet dram would not be enough. An old acquaintance, John Yorston, had a cot in Ardvik, and Tait hoped that if he called on him John might collect the neighbours to visit the Feas, and rejoice with them in receiving news of the well-being of their son in the far and unknown west.

Half-way down the hill a number of cattle grazed, small red and white beasts, and in a hollow a small human figure stood looking. As he approached, two other forms emerged from the hollow, and looked curiously at him. They stood motionless, side by side, each with a crooked stick which she carried when she drove the cattle to the hill in the morning and brought them home in the evening. They dropped their eyes as Tait drew near.

'Well, lasses,' he said, 'you'll soon be takin' the kye home.'

The girls looked shyly up, and then at one another. This silent conference over, the largest said, 'Yes, in a peerie while.'

'Which house is Nether Ardvik where the Feas live?'

'That one,' exclaimed all three, pointing to the middle-sized house south of the bay.

'And which cottage is John Yorston's?'

'That one,' all three answered, pointing to the third-nearest cot, which was newly thatched.

'Is he home, think you?'

'Aye,' said the smallest girl. 'He'll be flailing or doing something. He never stops.'

'Thanks, lasses,' said Tait, turning away.

'You'll be home from the Northwest?' The question shrilled after him from the middle-sized girl who had not yet had a chance of speaking alone.

Tait turned back. 'What makes you think that, lass?'

'You're brown like a peat.'

'No that brown, surely,' laughed Tait as he resumed his walk down the heather slope and on to the level stretch between the hill and the sea.

He passed the first two cottages, thinking how clean and neat they were compared to what they would have been when he left Orkney for Hudson's Bay. John Yorston's little row of buildings was particularly trim. Tait passed the kiln and entered the barn door. John was in the act of bringing the soople of his flail down on to the head of a sheaf lying on the raised threshing floor. He looked up on completing the stroke, and turned the sheaf with his foot and the hand staff.

'Bless me, Jamie Tait,' he exclaimed, leaning on the handstaff, the soople dangling from the thong that hinged the two parts of the flail together. 'Wait a minute and I'll be done.'

Yorston bent as he raised the flail, swayed, and brought it down on the head of the sheaf. Again and again he swung; he turned the sheaf and swung again. Only when he had swept the threshed oats into a pile did he turn again to his visitor.

'Weel, Jamie, it's good to see you safe home again. I hear you bought the farm in Orphir.'

'Aye, John. It took me many a weary year out west, and

cost me many a hungry belly, but we have our folks' farm back again.'

'That's grand, Jamie. But I tell you, I've made as much workin' and savin' on this bit o' ground here as some have done goin' Northwest or after the whales. It took you fifteen years?'

'Aye, John. Our ground is more than yours, but you'll add to it some day.'

'I hope to. But what brings you here all the way from Orphir? You'll be seeing' the Feas, I think.'

'Aye, John, and I'd like you and the neighbours to come wi' me. I have news the Feas will no like.'

'Women, I warrant. William's got an Indian wife, too?'

'That's it, John, and I'm dubious o' Walter Fea.'

'He'll no like it. Did William pay the father much for this wife o' his?'

'He paid nothing. No father was around. They have a boy comin' six, and Willie wants to send him home.'

'Walter'll no like that either,' said Yorston slowly. 'We'll make him hearty for you, however. You have a bottle?'

'Oh, aye. I would no come without it.'

'I have one, and so does Tammie Isbister, and Mrs Louttit has strong ale for the harvest home. We'll gather the neighbours after day-set.'

3

The Packy Woman

In the barn at Nether Ardvik, the young folks, having exhausted themselves dancing for a time, were seated on plank seats, each girl on the knee of her partner. The small tub of toddy went round, one effect of which was to increase the perspiration of each individual. At a table Mrs Louttit and Mrs Isbister dispensed bread and cheese, and strong ale in horn glasses.

Suddenly flashes of lightning lighted up the open barn doors, and these were followed by claps of thunder. Then came the rain in a heavy downpour.

James Tait took courage during a silence to speak with the Feas. He had already assured them that William was well. Now he described the hardships of cold and hunger, and the loneliness of the men far away from home and kindred.

'Poor William,' murmured Mrs Fea. 'He could die there for months and we would never know.'

'William has someone to look after him,' said Tait in desperation. 'He has taken an Indian wife, and they have a boy coming six.'

Walter Fea's bearded lips set in a hard line, but he said nothing.

'Oh, my!' exclaimed Mrs Fea. 'He'll be bringin' them home.'

'I'll no have that heathen woman and her bairn here,' growled Walter Fea.

'William thought you might not, and said he would never darken your door again if you didn't. His contract ends in 1797 and he'll buy a croft on another island.'

'Oh, Walter,' pleaded Mrs Fea, 'William's your own flesh and blood. You can't turn him off. I'll tell the lass about our Saviour, and I'll have the boy learn his bonie-words. Let William bring them home.'

'She's no comin' here; nor is her bairn.'

'Your very grandson, Walter. Your boy's boy, and bone o' your bone.'

'My son and grandson,' said Fea slowly, as the chatter and laughing resumed with the easing of the rain. 'Wife, I did no think o' that.'

Nothing was said for a time, as Tait and Mrs Fea looked anxiously at the old man's stern face. At last he said through clenched teeth, 'Let the boy come.' He paused; 'but no that savage woman,' he shouted.

A loud peal of thunder rent the air as if to emphasise Fea's ruling, and the chatter and laughing stopped suddenly, as if the whole crowd had heard and were shocked by the finality of his sentence. But all eyes were turned to the barn door, in which the small, ragged form of a woman had appeared with the last thunderclap. A bundle hung down from one shoulder. Her high-pitched voice shrilled through the barn.

'A grand night ye're havin' wi' scones and ale, and wi' Walter Fea gettin' news o' his son that he does no like too well. I tell thee, Fea, thoo'll get word thoo'll like worse. I saw that son o' thine lyin' dead on the ground, wi' Magnus Annal and Hugh Brough forbye, and the backs o' their heads riven off by a band o' nigh-naked savages. That's a fine thing to make merry about.'

Iron-grey hairs straggled down from the edge of a

tattered shawl and dropped water on to her weather-beaten and sunken cheeks on both sides of a beak-like nose, and down over her lantern jaws. Large dark eyes gleamed in their sockets. A cloak hung down in tatters to wrinkled grey stockings, and to the worn sheepskin rivlins she had on her feet. She stood slightly swaying, her head turning like that of a bird's to note each one in the barn.

'Old Nellie, the packy. Touched again!' So the whisper went round.

'You saw them, Nellie,' said Walter Fea at last. 'How could you see them thousands o' miles away?'

'I saw them in me mind, and it was on the blessed night o' Johnsmas.'

'Oh, aye,' mumbled John Yorston. 'Midsummer madness!'

'You do well, old woman, to say Johnsmas,' said James Tait. 'I tell you that I left William Fea and the other two safe in the fort wi' old Indian men, and the squaws and bairns who would harm nobody, six weeks before.'

'That I dunno' gainsay. I'm no tellin' ye about afore Johnsmas.'

'Well,' continued Tait, 'why did you not come in June? Why wait till late October?'

'Old Nellie has her bread to get,' answered the woman plaintively, 'selling bits o' cloth and ribbons, and needles and pins. I went to South Ronaldsay to tell the Annals, and I took ill there for weeks. Then I got to Orphir in a boat, and trudged to St Ola to tell the Broughs, and on here to tell thee, Walter Fea. Now ye'll no believe me, and I'll shake the dust o' your place from me rivlins.'

'No much dust will shake out on a night like this,' said a voice as the old packy woman turned to go.

'Nellie,' called Walter Fea.

The tiny, ragged figure turned.

'I lay little by your vision, old wife, but rest here in the barn this night. It's wild out, and you'll be warm here, and dry. Give her a bite to eat and a sup o' ale, Mrs Louttit.'

'Thank you, Walter Fea,' shrilled the old crone. 'I'll drink o' the ale, and I'll be glad to take the bread and cheese wi' me; but old Nellie must wander, and she'll never be beholden to others for a roof ower her head.'

She grasped a full horn glass and drained it. Mrs Isbister hastened to fill it again, and Nellie drained it once more. She took the bread and cheese Mrs Louttit offered, which she placed in the folds of her tattered shawl. At the door she turned, curtsied to the company, and went out into the night.

'Poor old body! Her wits are wandering again,' was said, but a shadow seemed to have fallen, and soon the crowd began to leave, all assuring the Feas that old Nellie was fey.

'You'll stay the night wi' us, Jamie Tait,' said Walter Fea.

'Thanks, but John is an old friend, and I promised to stay wi' him. Don't worry about the old wife. No Hudson's Bay man has been harmed by the Indians all the time I was there.'

The Feas stood uneasily for a time, and at last Walter said what Tait wanted to hear, looking at him from under bushy eyebrows. 'William can come here wi' his wife and bairn. Can you get that word to him?'

'Grand,' said Tait. 'Yes, I'll send word wi' the ship next summer. You'll find little Willie a fine lad but quiet and not forthcoming till he's well acquainted.'

4

Grandson

Almost a year after old Nellie's tale of her vision, the Feas started from Stromness by cart. Mr Tomison had written to them during the winter from London, and had assured them that their grandson would be coming when the Hudson's Bay ship returned in autumn. The miles of rutted road which wound between hills and around lochs had tired them, and it was with relief that they neared the town. Mrs Fea was anxious to see the boy; her husband, little as he believed old Nellie's story, was uneasy. At the crest of the hill north of the town they saw a barque anchored in Stromness Roads.

'Drive faster, Walter,' urged Mrs Fea. 'The little boy will be all by himsel'.'

'No, Jessie, for my cousin is seeing to him.' Fea did, however, prod the horse to a trot, muttering, 'My heart's no in this affair.' Soon he drew up at his cousin's house in the one narrow street that formed the town. Before they got off the cart, John Stockan came to meet them, his short body thin and shrivelled, his pale face solemn.

'How are you, John, and is our boy here?' asked Mrs Fea excitedly.

'Drive round to the back, Walter,' mumbled Stockan, and led the way. The Feas followed, both uneasy now. They got off the cart.

'What's the matter, John? Is the boy no here?' Mrs Fea demanded.

Stockan did not look at her, but on the ground. 'Walter, boy,' he said in a whisper, 'the Indians have killed your son along wi' Hugh Brough and Magnus Annal.'

Mrs Fea drew in her breath sharply. Both stood silent and still.

'My heart goes out to you both,' muttered Stockan, as he looked on the ground. 'Your one bairn!'

The Feas did not reply. At last Mrs Fea asked, 'And his bairn?'

'He got away wi' the one man no killed. He's in the house.'

Mrs Fea started towards it.

'Just a minute, Jessie. The boy's like a frightened foal ta'en from its mother. He'll no speak, and hardly eats, and the men on the ship said he had been like that all the voyage.'

'My poor boy!' Mrs Fea cried, and went to the door where John's wife was standing.

'It's a sad world this, Jessie,' she said.

'Aye!' Mrs Fea pushed past her and saw standing near the wall a boy, about seven, in buckskin dress. his face drawn and pinched, a far-away look in his dark eyes.

'Oh, Willie, Willie. Your own grandmother's come for you, boy.'

The boy shrank into the corner. Mrs Fea stood looking.

'Come me bairn. You're comin' home wi' me and your grandfather.'

The boy looked as if he did not hear or did not understand. He stared at her with wary eyes. Walter Fea, spare and tall like his son, came and stood by his wife, looking at the boy, whose dark eyes cleared, as they looked. A flash of expression, almost of recognition, came into them as the boy looked at his grandfather.

Walter Fea went forward confidently and put a hand on the boy's shoulder, the boy watching his face. Then he put his arm round the child, who turned to his grandfather and clasped him round the waist. Walter Fea lifted him and sat down in a large straw-backed chair, and put the boy on his knee. Little Willie buried his face in his grandfather's chest, breathing sobs.

Mrs Fea moved to go over to them. 'Leave them alone just now, Jessie,' whispered Stockan. 'Wife, set the table.'

'Aye, John, that boy must eat if he is to live,' answered Mrs Stockan, and went to the press for scones and butter, and ale. She put the kettle on the hook over the open fire, and with a bellows blew the smouldering peats to flame, for she decided to brew some of her precious tea in the hope the boy would like it. While her husband and Mrs Fea watched the two in the chair, Walter Fea sat looking out of the one small window, his arms around his grandson, whose face was still buried in his breast. When all was ready, Walter said, 'Come, Willie boy, we must eat before we take the road home.'

The boy rose, sat beside his grandfather at the table, and took a buttered scone his grandmother handed him. He watched his grandfather, and when he saw him eating, he began, eating slowly at first as if he had difficulty in swallowing, but, after a mouthful of ale, he ate freely, continuing as long as his grandfather, taking the scones from his grandmother's hand, and the horn-glass of ale, and stopping when his grandfather stopped. The frightened look left his face, and as he looked at the others from time to time, the pinched features relaxed. They did not speak, letting him get used to their presence. He refused the offered tea for his grandfather had refused it. When they all rose from the table, he turned to his grandmother and asked, 'We go . . .' His father's word came to him. 'We go home now?'

'Soon, Willie boy, when your grandfather's got the cart.'

Little Willie went with his grandfather for the cart. Soon he was seated between his grandparents, and the Stockans said their good-byes. The cart began its long journey up the slope on its way to Ardvik.

For a time, the boy watched each side of the road, his eyes and head turning constantly. As they rumbled over the ruts by the side of a long lake, Mrs Fea felt the little body relax. The boy's head dropped against his grandmother. She lifted him on to her lap, clasping him tight, and he slept as they went their way, past lochs, between hills, and at last by the sea. He was still asleep when they came to Nether Ardvik. Walter Fea took him gently from his wife, carried him into the house, and laid him on the bed in the closet room which had been made ready for him.

5

The Tattoos

His grandparents warned Kitty, the maid, and John Matches, the ploughman, to wait until Willie came to them and not go to him until they saw he did not fear them. For some days, Willie looked at Kitty and John with questioning in his dark eyes, and kept his distance. During the morning he kept close to his grandmother, and in the afternoons he dogged his grandfather's footsteps. There came a morning when Kitty saw he was watching her feed the hens with some interest; she handed him the basket of corn, saying, 'Throw them some, Willie.' He did so, and Kitty called his attention to different hens, the good layers. John Matches, taking in the last of the harvest, saw him look with eagerness into the cart. 'Climb up, Willie, and tramp them down for me.' Willie did so, rode to the yard on the load, and tramped the sheaves in the stack with vigour.

His grandparents thought, however, that the boy still seemed tense, turning round suddenly for no reason. Walter Fea and Willie were one day standing with their backs to the low stone wall that enclosed the pasture, when the foal galloped up, its little hoofs thudding. Walter Fea found Willie pressed close to him, and felt him shake. When he lifted the boy up, Willie stared over his shoulder and stopped quivering. He had seen the foal had no rider. His grandfather turned around, set him down, and showed

him how to scratch the foal's ears. One morning shortly
after, some cottar set fire to a patch of heather on the
hillside, to get it ready for cultivation. The smoke drifted
in a cloud down to Nether Ardvik. In the yard, Willie
ran to his grandmother in terror. She saw his eyes roll as
he looked at the smoke. 'Aye, Willie,' she said soothingly,
'it will no come here. Some poor body burning a patch of
heather to make a field. Never fear, my boy.' Willie
watched the cloud roll past some distance away, and the
fear left his face.

Then one day a white-headed boy, smaller than Willie,
came with a little pail to get some buttermilk for his
mother. 'Willie, you and peerie Mansie go out and play
till Kitty gets the churning finished.' Willie went, and
Mansie walked with him. Willie did not speak or look at
the boy. Then he heard a piping voice say, 'You've got
far more hens than us. A hundred or more, Willie.' They
went on, Willie still quiet, and came to the pasture, where
three calves looked at them, turned round, kicked up
their heels, and went galloping off, tails up. Mansie
laughed; Willie joined in as the calves came galloping
back. 'You have three calves. I think that red and white
one bonny. We just have one and it's brown.' Willie
answered 'I like that one, too.' After that the boys talked
freely until Mrs Fea called Mansie. After he left, Mrs Fea
asked, 'Do you like peerie Mansie, Willie?'

'Aye, Grandmother. He says we have a hundred hens.'

'No that many, Willie.'

'And he likes our red and white calf.'

'Well, that's grand.'

As the Feas went to bed that night Walter said, 'I
think, Jessie, our boy is losing that frightened furled-up
look he had.'

'Aye, he has, Walter. It's *our* hens and *our* calves wi' him now.'

Another boy called with his mother shortly after. While Mrs Merriman went in the house to talk with Mrs Fea, Willie and her boy Geordie, older and heavier than Willie, went to see Walter Fea use the flail in the barn. It was a common sight to Geordie, who sat on the straw, picked up a handful, straightened it out and began to twist it into a straw rope. Willie watched him with interest. Walter Fea took note. 'Show Willie how to make simmons, Geordie.'

Geordie held out a length of the straw rope, and said, 'Take a handful like this, Willie. Twist it here. Then add thinner bits to each end as you get it twisted. Like this.' He handed the started bit to Willie, and let him twist, showing him how to add the extra lengths so that it was a continuous rope.

Willie started slowly, gradually picked up speed, and began to twist with vigour. 'What do you use it for?' he asked Geordie.

'To thatch the stacks so that they don't blow over, and to thatch the roof, like that on the byre, Willie.'

'And what do you call it?'

'Simmons, Willie, simmons.'

The boys talked as they twisted, until Geordie was called by his mother. 'Willie soon learns, Mr Fea,' he said.

'Let me see. So he does,' said Willie's grandfather.

So Willie had made one more friend. There were few children near him, and children had to work most of the time, gleaning, and gathering potatoes in the autumn, spreading seaweed on the fields in winter, herding in spring and summer. Parents had told their children to be good to little Willie who had had such an awful time of it. The few he saw were good, but shy of this boy who had come from so far away and suffered so much. In spring 1796, however, six months after coming to Ardvik, Willie started to go to the kirk school along with Mansie Isbister and Geordie Merriman who started at the same time. The three got on well with the few other children, and with their teacher, Mr Rendall. Willie's strangeness to the children had worn off by this time, but as no others were in his class, Mansie and Geordie were his very own friends. In their first year they received special attention from the schoolmaster. But in the second, all three found themselves in trouble for the first time. They were told to stay behind one day when the other children were dismissed.

Hew Rendall, came in through the low door of the little building after seeing the other pupils starting for home. The rough wooden door creaked dismally to the three boys as he shut it behind him. He spoke to the eldest first. 'George Merriman, why were you late this morning?'

Geordie looked at his feet, looked up and down again, stammered, and was silent.

'Magnus Isbister, why were you late?'

The little fair-haired boy looked straight at his teacher. 'Geordie fell in the burn and Willie and me pulled him out,' he piped. 'Then we had to wring out his troosers.'

'With him in them?'

'No, we had an awful job pullin' them off, for they stuck to him.'

The boys were relieved to see a smile on the master's craggy features. 'Was this at the stepping stones?' he asked.

'No,' piped Magnus quickly, 'higher up. Willie and me jumped clean ower, but Geordie fell in.'

'Why did you not cross at the stones which were on your way?'

B

None of the boys answered. Geordie shuffled uneasily.

'William Fea, why were you not coming at the crossing?'

The dark eyes of the boy had never left his teacher's face. 'Old Nellie was standing at the crossing, and we were feared.'

'Old Nellie! Come, come. Don't tell me you were afraid of her.'

'She had a needle in her hand, Mr Rendall, and was goin' to stick it in us,' mumbled Geordie, his eyes rolling.

'Now, what did you do to her? Out with it.'

'I cried something to her first,' admitted Magnus.

'Cried what?'

The little boy turned his head away and mumbled

> *Nellie Nellie Nornie*
> *Sister o' auld Horney.*

'What?' thundered the master. 'And did you two boys join in?'

'Yes, sir,' answered William Fea, 'after she came out and we had run away.'

The schoolmaster looked black. He jerked open a drawer and took out a leather strap, the five tails hanging down stiffly. The three boys eyed him in fear. Not one of them had ever been strapped. He looked at them fiercely for a minute. 'No, this won't do,' he muttered to himself. Aloud he said, 'Next time you'll taste leather. Now, you'll come with me to Nellie, and she will use the needle on you, and mark you for life, so that you will never forget this day.'

He put the strap away, and turned smiling to the boys. They now understood what Old Nellie did with her needle, and it was not so terrible.

'She'll tattoo a snake on me, I hope,' piped Magnus.

'She will choose. Get some peats from the pile to take
to her; Magnus three yellow, Willie three brown, and
George three blue.'

The boys did so, packing the peats into the compartment
of their satchels in which they carried a peat each day for
the school fire. The other compartment held their Bibles,
some sheets of brown paper, a small slate, and some thin
lengths of slate got from a near-by quarry and used as
slate pencils. Off they went, the boys trotting at times to
keep up with Hew Rendall's long strides. They crossed the
ayre, the stony beach at the mouth of the burn, and walked
along the sand to a rough track up a rocky bank, and in
single file along a footpath on the commons to a slope
down the low cliffs which bounded Ardvik on the north.
A short way down lay old Nellie's dwelling, for she
wandered no more. The aft half of an old boat had been
set on a low foundation of beach stones, and the sea end
built up with stones round a low door now open to the
April sun. Nellie, clad in tattered homespuns, sat on a
large stone, her sprettos or footless stockings fastened to
her big toes with leather thongs, her wrinkled and hard
rivlins on the ground.

'God be wi' thee, Nellie.'

'And wi' thee, Hew Rendall. The three peerie boys are
white about the gills, I see.'

The three boys were looking at Nellie with some fear
as her black eyes held first one and then the other.

'Yes, and you know why, Nellie,' continued Hew Rendall. 'But they've brought thee some peats. Give Nellie
the peats, boys.'

Nellie spoke as each boy put the peats beside her.

'Yellow for a quick flame. God be wi' thee, Mansie

Isbister. Brown to boil the pot. God be wi' thee, Willie Fea. And three blue to keep the fire in a' the night. God be wi' thee, Geordie Merriman.'

'I want thee, Nellie, to put a mark on them so they'll mind no to be late for school,' said Hew Rendall.

'Aye, aye,' murmured Nellie, looking at each boy in turn. She went into her boat-domed home and returned with a vial of blue liquid and a needle.

'Thee, first, Geordie Merriman,' she said from her seat on the stone. 'Sit on the ground here, and give me thee arm.'

Geordie shuffled forward and sat down by the old woman.

'Stop shaking, Geordo. I'll no kill thee, boy. I'm pittin' a heart on thee for thoo're a boy o' good heart.'

Geordie set his teeth as the needle started pricking into his skin, and the other boys watched eagerly as the blue double outline of a heart took shape on the underside of his forearm. Geordie, finding the ordeal not so painful as he had expected, said, 'Don't be feared, boys. It's no sore.'

'I'm no frightened,' declared Magnus. 'Thoo were.'

Having finished with Geordie, Nellie said, 'Thee, next, Willie Fea. I'll put an anchor on thee. I saw thee runnin' when the Indians killed thee father.'

'Ayek was running,' corrected Willie. 'I was lyin' still in the grass.'

'That was wise. The birds and beasts all learn that.'

'What's the anchor for?' asked Willie.

'Thoo'll drift for a long time, boy, but thee anchor will grip some day and hold thee.'

Willie looked at her strangely, but asked no more. When the anchor was complete on his forearm, Nellie said, 'Now thee, peerie Mansie. I'll pit a cross on thee. Dunno ask why.'

Magnus felt disappointed he was not to get a snake, but he watched with interest until the cross was complete.

'There, boys,' said Hew Rendall, 'don't be late again, for there's no more marks for you. And you'll aye be good to Nellie.'

'I choosed to wander,' mumbled the old woman, 'and it was fine for many a day. Now I'm no fit, and take it as it comes. The peerie boys will have their own trials wi' the years.'

The teacher turned to go, and each boy thanked old Nellie, and followed along the beach.

When they parted at the stony mouth of the burn Hew said, 'Show your marks to the young men. They'll come to have their initialled hearts linked with those of their lasses, and may live to regret the groat they paid old Nellie. I hope you three boys will never have to wander weary, cold, and hungry as she has had to do.'

Willie turned homeward. He would drift for a long time, old Nellie had said, and a sudden chill had come over him. It lasted only a moment. There was no sudden danger here to leap out of nowhere at him or at his grandparents, or at his friends and Hew Rendall. His grandfather's house came in sight, square and permanent. But he did not think of it now as only his grandfather's house. He entered his own home, and showed his blue anchor to his grandmother.

6

Candlemas

Willie Fea had been given a birthday. His grandfather, worried that he did not know the boy's exact age, had written to William Tomison of the Hudson's Bay Company early in 1798, and Tomison, getting the letter while he was down at Hudson's Bay from the interior in July, had replied by the same ship. It reached Ardvik in October. Little Willie was born at Cumberland House on the Saskatchewan in 1789 in the month of February, but the exact day was unknown. The Feas had consulted with Mr Peace, the minister, and had fixed on a date near Candlemas, February 15, for Willie's birthday.

In honour of his tenth birthday, a Tuesday, Mrs Fea prepared a feast, and invited Willie's two friends, Magnus and Geordie, over for the afternoon. The boys watched Kitty, the servant girl, and Mrs Fea cut up the suet, dust the raisins and currants with flour, add spices, salt, flour and water, stir all together in a pan and shape the damp mixture to a big round ball. Then Mrs Fea wrapped it in a white cloth, put it in a big pot, and set it on the stove to boil.

'Now, boys, it will be three hours boilin'. Go out o' our way for that time. This is gyro night and you can get ready for it.'

'I've never got out on gyro night, for my mother says the gyro will get me,' Magnus piped.

'Gyro?' questioned Willie.

'Just an old tale, Willie,' explained his grandmother. 'A muckle woman comes out o' the sea when she sees the fire the bairns have made, and she chases the small boys wi' a seaweed tangle.'

'A muckle woman? Does she live in the sea?'

'That's the old story, Willie. Long ago, afore our Saviour came the folks thought that queer things came out o' the sea at the changes o' the year, and they made fires so that the monsters could no seize them.'

'Does this gyro hit the boys?'

'That she does. If she gets near thee she'll make thee jump.'

'I'm takin' care she does no catch me,' declared Geordie. 'Last year she was near on me when she tripped ower her long skirts.'

'A good job for thee, Geordie,' chimed in Magnus, 'the way thoo lunders along.'

'Was she very big?' asked Willie, his eyes shifting rapidly from speaker to speaker.

'Twice me size,' Geordie informed him.

'Ach, Willie, it's just one o' the big boys or sometimes two o' them dressed up in a woman's clothes wi' simmons tied aboot them; thoo kens simmons, the straw ropes that thatch the stacks. It's just a game, but the old folks believed in the gyro. Awa now wi' you and get ready for her.'

'Aye, Mrs Fea, we'll go to the hill to get heather for the fire and our torches, and could we take some peats?' asked Geordie.

The three boys ran out and kept running by the burn until they came to the Muckle Pow. Out of breath, they went slowly to the Peerie Pow where the heather grew long, and pulled bunches of it. Loaded with heather, they went down the burn, and met three slightly older boys going up.

'We've started a pile on the stones at the mouth of the burn,' cried Frank Tait, 'so stack yours on that. Come back for more.'

'Who's the gyro for the night?' enquired Geordie.

'The big boys are no tellin',' answered Charlie Matches. 'Are you gettin' any peats?'

'Mrs Fea said we could take some,' said Magnus.

'That's grand. We'll make a blaze,' said Frank, and the boys went on.

Down on the stones just above tide mark a boy was shaping the pile, dry grass underneath, some straw, and some heather.

'She'll be a grand fire, Davie,' said Geordie, as they laid down their burdens.

'Aye, and will burn long if we get some peats.'

'We're bringin' some, Davie,' Magnus hurried to say.

'Well, get them now, and then get your torches. I'll have heather enough when the other boys get back. The darkness will be on us soon.'

The three boys walked back to Nether Ardvik for the peats. Loaded with four large ones each, they returned to the mouth of the burn, where Davie Craigie was surrounded by six small boys.

'Boy,' exclaimed Charlie Matches, 'this should draw a gyro or two out o' the sea.'

'Take care she'll no pull thee into it,' said Davie.

'No fear, for I'll singe her wi' me torch.'

'Mebbe, if she does no first clout thee ower the head. Now, get your torches or it'll be dark.'

When the three boys had returned to the stackyard of

Nether Ardvik, they arranged their bundles of heather to make torches, Geordie twisting straw round the butts of the bundles to make handgrips, and then they went into the kitchen. The smell of cooking suet, flour and fruit permeated the room. Steam shot from the lid of the pot, and the plate on which the dumpling rested gurgled as it rose up and down.

'It's about ready, boys,' said Mrs Fea, 'and we're just waitin' for thee grandfather, Willie, and for Johnny Matches to come in. It's ower dark for them to work now. Are you a' ready for the gyro?'

'Aye, Mrs Fea,' said Geordie, 'and a grand fire she'll be.'

The two men came in, and all seated themselves on straw-bottomed chairs round the large table. Walter Fea said grace. Then he added, 'This is the first birthday our grandson's ever celebrated wi' us, and may he have every other one here as long as we live, and many more besides.'

'Many o' them, Willie,' said the company.

Willie brightened with pleasure on hearing his grandfather's words, but felt sheepish when all eyes were on him. He was glad when Kitty placed the large dumpling, twice the size it had been, in front of his grandmother. Mrs Fea cut generous slices, and when all were served, Walter Fea began, the others following. The boys ate and ate, and after the third helping, Mrs Fea asked if they were full now.

'I'm full right up,' declared Magnus.

'So am I,' said Willie.

'Me stummick is,' said Geordie, 'but I'm no full right up.'

Geordie looked surprised when the others laughed.

'Never mind them, Geordo,' said Mrs Fea. 'Pass thee plate and I'll fill thee full to the neck.'

When Geordie was finished, the boys went to get their torches, Magnus and Willie keen on the night's adventure, Geordie walking slowly, as he had been at the fire last year, and also because he was full to the neck.

'Come on, Geordie,' admonished Willie, 'or we'll miss the lighting.'

'We would no miss much. Run on and I'll come at me own gait.'

The two ran on, the sliver of the first new moon of spring giving a little light. Soon after they got to the burn, Davie Craigie ignited the fire with flint and tinder, and the two pressed near where the other little boys stood. As the smoke billowed around them Magnus cried out, for Willie had grasped his arm. When his arm was released, Magnus gripped it with his other hand, for it hurt, and staggered out of the smoke, choking. 'Mighty, Willie,' he cried, 'thee nail marks must be deep in me arm.' But Willie was not there. 'Willie,' called Magnus, 'where has thoo got to?'

He listened, and heard a faint 'Here.'

'Well, come to the fire.' Getting no answer he went to the sound, and found Willie crouched in long weeds and grass.

'What's the matter, Willie. Did thoo see the gyro?'

'The smoke,' gasped Willie.

'Mighty, boy, the reek will no burn thee; the fire does that. Come on.'

Magnus took hold of Willie's arm, and tried to drag him to the fire, now smoking heavily, but Willie held back. Geordie came by. 'Geordie, Willie's feared o' the reek. Help me to drag him to it.'

'Ach, Willie, come on and stop bulderin',' said Geordie. thinking Willie was putting on an act. Willie, seeing the timid Geordie go forward unconcernedly, followed in his slow footsteps to the fire where some thin tongues of flame pierced the smoke. Mansie ran in front, and just as Willie and Geordie came up, he grabbed Willie, and lay down in a billow of smoke, pulling Willie over him. Willie struggled hard to free himself, but Magnus held on, while both choked on the smoke. They let go their holds, the smoke passing over, and both still coughing. Then both sat up laughing, and gazed at the blazing fire.

'Come on, baith o' you,' said Geordie, 'and light your torches. The gyro will be here afore you ken it.'

Willie was over his fright. He ran forward with Mansie, and lit his torch. Nine little boys with torches started hopping in a circle around the fire, chanting

Gyro, guy, Gyro guy!
Come and catch me. I'll no fly.

A yell rang out, and from seaward came a blur beyond the firelight. As it approached, the boys saw a black-masked face, a woman's shawl on its head from which hung strings of seaweed. The body was girded with simmons, as were the legs below a woman's old skirt. Another yell rang out, and the gyro raised an arm flourishing a long and supple tangle, the largest seaweed stem to be found. It made a dash at the circle of boys who broke and ran in all directions. Magnus and Willie, running near one another, heard Geordie give a howl, and then another.

'He would fill himself to the neck,' said Magnus in disgust.

The two dashed to the howling Geordie with blazing torches, and just as the gyro was about to hit Geordie again, Willie ran between, taking the swish across his back, ran on, and turned to laugh at the gyro. It ran at

him, and the three boys with two others ran back to the
fire. As they ran around it, another gyro came from the
sea, and caught Magnus a clout that made him yell, and
as it raised the tangle again, Willie again ran between,
taking the blow aimed at Magnus, and again turned
round to laugh. Both gyros advanced on the group of boys,
who scattered; one followed some boys up along the burn,
the other vainly tried to get a blow in on the elusive Willie,
who darted near and away. Magnus, trying also to dart
near, got hit across the neck, and Willie darted in again
to take its attention. The torches of other boys were now
moving slowly across a field, the gyros tiring, and also the
boys, and the torches burning low. The chant came:

> *Gyro guy, gyro guy!*
> *Queek noo or the fire will die.*
> *Thoo'll no get thee to the sea*
> *Afore it sloaks; thoo can't catch me.*

The efforts of both gyros were now feeble, their arms and
legs weary. The fire was dying down, the torches burning
low. One by one they spluttered, the sparks floating away
and dying. 'Barlow, barlow' was shouted, signifying that
the crier was no longer in the game, and one by one the
boys wandered back to the fire, now with only the peats
burning with low flames. The gyros wandered down to
the sea, and as the little boys waited for them to return in
ordinary garb, a series of high-pitched yells sounded, and
much giggling as a line of six big girls ran towards the
fire.

'Lasses!' came from the gyro's voice down on the beach.
'They've no right here. After them, boys!'

The boys, spent with running ran yelling after the big
girls who broke and ran in different directions, and then

converged on the fire, leaping over the flames one by one. The little boys tried to chase them away, waiting until they leapt over the fire, but failed. After jumping three times over, the girls ran up along the burn, easily out-distancing the little boys.

'The jads!' exclaimed Charlie Matches. 'Can't wait for Johnsmas, but must steal our night.'

The fire was almost out. 'Come on home, boys,' said Geordie to Magnus and Willie. 'That's a', and me insides are like to burst.'

'And no wonder,' said Magnus, as the three moved away to separate outside Nether Ardvik.

'Well, Willie boy, did thoo have a grand night?' greeted Mrs Fea.

'Aye, Grannie, it was grand but I was frightened o' the smoke at first.'

'The reek, Willie. It'll no harm thee.'

'Aye, I ken that now, but I swallowed an awful lot o' it first.'

'The gyro did not get thee, then?'

'Aye he did, three times.'

'Did he hurt thee?'

'A little. It was nothing.'

'A wallop o' a heavy tangle nothing. Boy, boy!'

7

Red Waistcoat

Three more Candlemas dumplings had been eaten, and spring had passed into summer, summer into autumn, and the corn was ready for the scythe. Geordie Merriman, now a rather stout boy of fifteen, no longer went to school. Although he had learned to read and write, he found further studies difficult, and he was needed at home to help on the small farm of his parents, and to take seasonal work with big farmers for some money. Willie, now thirteen, and Magnus still went to school, but school was closed for six weeks so that the children could help in harvesting the corn and the potatoes. Most of the young men were away from home, many press-ganged into the navy or army, some serving on whalers and on merchant ships, others in the service of the Hudson's Bay in far-off Rupert's Land.

Walter Fea had hired Geordie to help in the gathering of the harvest. He had also hired Magnus Isbister, now a slight lad of twelve, his hair still snow-white. Willie Fea was happy to work in his grandfather's fields with his two friends, with his grandparents and Kitty the maid and John Matches.

Willie had grown into a tall, slim, close-knit lad, swifter and more athletic than any of his companions. He was dark-complexioned, his hair jet black, and his dark brown eyes forever taking note of the tracks of birds or hares.

These dark eyes could go expressionless very quickly when the boy was faced with something he did not understand, something strange and unfamiliar. His grandparents were very proud when Hew Rendall told them he was the most promising scholar he had ever had, and Walter Fea was determined to have the boy educated so that he could become a teacher, or a minister even. As he liked his studies and his teacher, Willie did not often work on the farm, but the lives of the household and of others depended on the harvest being gathered. The long war had made it impossible to get food that the farm and the sea did not supply. In the cornfield of Nether Ardvik, Walter Fea and his wife, John Matches, Kitty and the three boys laboured to get the crop scythed, bound into sheaves, and set up in stooks.

One day, when the sun stood over the southern hump of the Fiold, Mrs Fea and Kitty left the men and boys working to go and get breakfast, as the midday meal was called. The next half-hour was hard work for the boys. Rain was threatening, and the two men kept on scything until the sun had passed the hump. Then John Matches laid down his scythe and helped the boys, for every cut stalk had to be gathered and bound before they left the field. At last Walter Fea, too, put down his scythe, the last sheaf was bound, and men and boys walked away, all ready for breakfast.

As the party went over the stile, the two men turned back to survey the area cut and bound, and the amount of standing grain still to be cut. Magnus and Willie compared the cracks and blisters on their hands. Their job was to twist bands and gather the scythed barley into sheaves, as the women did. Geordie and John Matches did the binding and the setting up of the sheaves.

'Your hands, Mansie, will get hard like mine when you're used to the work. Willie's got worse blisters.'

'Mine would no blister if I had a soft job like thine,' retorted Magnus, squeezing the moisture out of a blister.

'I hope we can finish this field before the rain comes,' Walter Fea said to John Matches.

'Well, it's coming,' said John. 'Now, what is peerie Annie in a steer about?'

Little Annie Tait, a girl from a neighbouring cot was hurrying up.

'Oh, Mr Fea,' she shrilled breathlessly, 'the press gang's comin', two men and one wi' a red waistcoat. Mother thinks they're after John.'

The two men looked at one another. Were the old men to be taken?

'And she says to tell them at the Ardvik cottages,' added Annie.

'Thanks, Annie,' said Walter Fea. 'Little time to hide, John. Lie down in the barley. Mansie, run down and tell John Yorston about this.'

As John Matches hunkered back over the stile to the barley field, Magnus raced off over the fields, full of his mission, for his two elder brothers had been forced into the navy.

'Annie, tell Mrs Fea to hold breakfast for us, and say you're to stay for breakfast, too.'

'Oh, thanks, Mr Fea,' cried Annie, her face lit up. 'I'll tell her.' The little girl ran off.

Walter Fea stood with the boys watching as two figures turned from the road into the cart track leading up to Nether Ardvik. Surely no one would press John Matches into the services, a man over forty who had never been a sailor or boatman. The two figures drew nearer, both big men; one, who walked with a limp, being particularly large.

'The constables carry sticks, Mr Fea,' said Geordie. 'Only one o' them has a stick.'

'Aye, Geordie, but they're up to every trick.'

'But the man in the red waistcoat is bigger than any constable in the parish, and the navy men wear blue,' added Geordie.

'We'll see in a minute, Geordie.'

The two men drew near, and the eyes of the watchers were on the big man in the red waistcoat. Willie felt a strange fear steal over him, a vague misgiving that he had seen this man before. The man's features were massive, his head big and square, his nose large and hooked, his face brown. Suddenly Willie knew him; Chief Tomison, who had come down the river to see the furs dispatched, and with whom James Tait and Ayek's father had gone away a few weeks before the Gros Ventres had come.

Walter Fea now recognised James Tait, the shorter man, whom he had not seen since the stormy night when old Nellie had announced the death of his son. Overcoming the feeling which this recognition renewed, he exclaimed, 'Jamie Tait! I'm glad to see thee.'

'And I'm glad to see thee well, Mr Fea. This is Mr Tomison.'

The two men, united by a common desire for Willie's well-being, shook hands, looking hard at one another. Then both turned away. Soon Tomison spoke hoarsely. 'Your son was a good man. My heart was sore for many a day, but what must be must be.'

'Aye,' muttered Fea, and an awkward silence followed.

Rain suddenly pelted down; Walter Fea pulled himself together and said, 'We're goin' in for breakfast, and the boys are starvin'. Come in wi' us, the both o' you, and have your breakfast wi' us.'

A breathless Magnus jumped over the dyke, having run to John Yorston with the news and back to get his breakfast. 'Oh, Mansie,' said Walter Fea, 'thoo had thee run for nothin'. It was Mr Tait and Mr Tomison comin' to see me. Run thee ower, Geordie, and tell John.' Geordie, having eaten nothing during five hours of work, set out wondering if he would collapse from hunger before getting back.

'Willie,' said his grandfather, 'tell John Matches to come out o' the corn. We thought you might be the constables, Mr Tomison.'

'Willie! Little Willie Fea!' muttered the big man. 'It's him I want to see.' Aloud he said, 'Where is the boy?'

Walter Fea looked around. No Willie was in sight. 'Bless me, where did the boy go? Run, Mansie, and tell John, and bring Willie too.'

Magnus jumped over the stile and shouted 'John! Johnny Matches! Come for breakfast. That was Jamie Tait and Mr Tomison.'

Matches raised himself from the barley, and Magnus shouted, 'Willie!' There was no answer. 'Did thoo see Willie go anywhere, John?'

'No me.'

'Where has he got to? Willie, Willie, Willie, Willie, Willie,' cried Magnus in a high voice as if he were calling the hens.

There was no answer, but John Matches noted a little gap in the barley, went to it, and found Willie lying on his face.

'Gid-gad, Willie, no press gang would be after thee,' said John. 'Mr Tomison will want to see thee.'

'I don't want to see him,' mumbled the boy.

'Lord, boy, thoo must. He'll set thee up for life. Come out o' the corn.'

Willie rose slowly. Magnus came over. 'Mighty, Willie, no press gang would take thee.'

'It's no that.'

'What is it then?'

'I don't ken.'

'Boy thoo're a queer one. First feared o' the reek, and now this. Next it will be the trolls.'

'I'm no feard o' trolls.'

'Stow, boys and come for breakfast. It's six hours since a morsel has gone down me rattle.'

The three went into the house where Walter Fea sat at the head of a long table, a guest at each side. Tomison rose. 'Little Willie!' He turned to Mrs Fea. 'I would have known him anywhere.' He extended a large hand, saying to Mrs Fea, 'He's the very spit of his father.'

'He is that,' agreed Mrs Fea, 'and walks just like him too.' Willie had gone slowly forward to take the hand offered him.

'Boy, the blisters on your hands. It's a wonder you can work,' Tomison said.

'He never heeds them,' Walter Fea boasted.

'Aye. He takes that of his mother's folk,' Tomison said in a low voice.

Willie was glad he could sit down by his grandmother, as far as he could get from the guests, who conversed with his grandfather. The boys, being hungry, ate steadily and silently. The sky darkened, and rain pelted against the small window.

'I doubt we cut no more this day,' said John Matches.

'Well, we have visitors, and me old bones can do wi' a

rest. John, thee and the boys can flail, and put Kitty to the quern, wife. I'm no the man I was, Mr Tomison, bein' near the allotted span.'

'I ken how you feel, Mr Fea. I'm sixty-five.'

'And you've had a hard life, Mr Tomison. It must be forty years since you first went to the Bay.'

'Forty-three years gone by, but I was home when you lost your boy. Thirty years in the heart of the country where the born gentlemen don't go.'

'Well, you're gentleman enough wi' a' you've done for the bairns in your island to get them some school to go to.'

'My day is past, Mr Fea, and I see my life's work ruined by men out to feather their own nests, ruining the Indians with rum, and not with the good of the Company at heart. And that's something I want to speak to you about.'

The Feas looked at one another. Mrs Fea said, 'Well, come on to the ben.'

The three left the flag-stoned kitchen for the wooden-floored room called the ben which had an armchair and settee, sheep-skin rugs, and curtains over a box bed in a recess. When they were seated, Tomison began abruptly.

'It's about Willie. I'll pay for his schooling for at least three more years. I would like him to go to the Company, in which I have influence yet to forward him.'

Walter Fea looked down and said nothing. Mrs Fea, having waited for her husband to speak, cried, 'We lost our one boy there. We're no losing his boy.'

Tomison stared in front of him for a time. Then he said, 'It gave me a sore heart, Mrs Fea. But it is as God wills it. Folks are losing sons all the time in the navy and in the fishing, no to speak of them that die of fever. We go when our time's up.'

Walter Fea spoke. 'Aye, we don't want to lose this boy, but it's no in our hands. You have helped already with his schoolin', Mr Tomison. I want him to get all o' that he can, but times are hard wi' us now. Do you help only if he promises to go to the Company?'

'No,' burst out Tomison. 'I'll help, as I've done wi' the bairns of my parish, only more for him. It's his mother's folk I'm thinking of. They're being ruined by drink traded by both companies, the Hudson's Bay and the Northwest, and will die out if this goes on. Willie could be a kind of missionary among them.'

'Fine he could be that same,' declared Mrs Fea. 'I learned him his bonie-words, and Mr Peace our minister has put him through all his catechism and much o' the Bible.'

'Jessie, woman, has thoo changed thee mind already? Think o' the boy,' her husband admonished.

'But, Walter, I'm thinkin' o' the word of God. We can't deny "Go ye into all the world and preach the Gospel."'

'True, Mrs Fea,' agreed Tomison readily. 'I never let a Sabbath go by without reading divine service to the men.'

'Well, Jessie and me have no gone or read.'

'We had no the learnin', Walter.'

'No. Well, Mr Tomison, you can speak to Willie, but he must no be asked for a promise. If he goes to the Company, it will be his choice.'

'I'll ask him for no promise, but I'll ask him if he would like to go to the Company.'

'Well, I'll send him in so you can speak to him.'

Ten years earlier, Tomison had put his hand on Willie's head, shortly before the boy's father was killed. Willie came in, remembering that large hand, and now went slowly forward, a tall slim lad to the stout old man who again held a gnarled hand out to him. Willie took it hesitatingly, his blistered hand still sore from the last grip.

'Sit down, Willie,' said Tomison, his gruff voice softened. 'I've been speaking to your grandfolks.'

Willie's dark eyes never left Tomison's face, but he said nothing.

'It's about your education, Willie. So you like your teacher?'

'Grand,' said the boy with feeling.

'And you would go on learning if you get the chance?'

'Aye.'

'That's fine. Mr Fea wants you to go on, may be to be a minister. Did you think of that?'

'No, and I don't think I'd like to be one.'

'How would you like to be an officer with the Hudson's Bay?'

'I'll no be that.'

'Mighty, boy. Why not?'

'The Indians killed my folks. If I go among them it will be to kill them.'

'Mercy, Willie, that's no right. The Good Book tells us to forgive. And the Indians you would be among are no the Gros Ventres that killed your folks.'

'I ken about the Good Book, but I remember me father's groans and me mother lying scalped, and I can't forget it.'

'Aye, it's no a thing one could forget. But you see me limp. A drunken Indian stabbed me in the leg and tried to kill me. I could have broken his back, but I put him out of the fort, and we were friends after.'

'Aye, but he was drunk.'

'So were the Gros Ventres when they were on the

warpath. They act like drunk men, and ken not what they do.'

'They should no have killed me folk.'

'But they were simply killing, not your folk only.'

'I don't want to see any Indians again.'

'Indians! Pedlars had given the Crees guns to fight the Gros Ventres. That's why the whites were killed. And the Indians in the post. Guns and rum! Ruination!'

Tomison was silent for a minute, then he said, 'You must think of something you want to do, Willie. Your grandfather's an old man, and if he went, the laird would not rent to a boy. Well, well. Keep on learning. I'll see you through even if Mr Fea lives on. But my heart's sore for your mother's folks, Willie.'

The big man rose and put his hand on Willie's shoulder. Willie felt like crying, but managed to say, 'Thank you, sir, for your kindness.'

'Your father, Willie, was aye a friend to me. God bless you, lad.'

8

The One Fea Left

At the end of 1804 Willie could no longer attend the kirk
school since it did not provide for pupils over the age of
fifteen. He went daily to the manse to be tutored by Mr
Peace, the minister, for three hours, and spent the rest of
his day either in study or in working on the farm. Some of
the work on the farm delighted him, the sowing, the
ploughing, and the harvesting, but he found work in the
byre and in the pig sty unpleasant. Yet this work was done
by Kitty, and by his grandmother, and on occasion by
John Matches. He felt badly when he saw his grandmother
do it, while he, clean and comfortable, sat at a book. His
grandmother was growing bent and breathless. Willie
noted her flushed face when she had been stooping over
for some time. He saw also that his grandfather was losing
his erect bearing and walked bent. He spoke to his grandfather about it.

'Grandfather, I'm going to stop home and work.'

Walter Fea looked taken aback. 'Bless me, Willie, do
you no like the work wi' Mr Peace?'

'It's not that. I like to study, but Grandmother and you
are out working in the cold and wet while I'm in here
warm and clean.'

'Boy, Willie, do you no think we would miss it if we
did not have it to do? It's all we've ever known, and we'll
do it till we drop.'

'But I should be doing more. I could work for half the day.'

'You work enough to please us. You keep to your books, for proud we are that you are a scholar. It's a grand thing to have in the family, and it would be sore on us if you stopped.'

Willie pondered this for a time. His grandfather spoke again.

'Your father, Willie, wanted you to learn. That's why he was so anxious to get you home. We must not forget that, Willie.'

Willie did not say anything more. His grandfather had spoken of his father's wish as something final. He did work more on the farm, and yet he kept at his studies. Since Tomison's visit, over two years before, he had occasionally worried over what he would do in order to live, but he could not come to a decision. There seemed to be three occupations open, teacher, minister, and writer or notary; and no one attracted him more than the other. Meanwhile, he did not have to decide; his education was arranged, and there was plenty to do on the farm. The failing health of his grandparents worried him more. He felt that the farm was not paying as it once did, for his grandfather occasionally engaged an additional man but only for a short time, although the man's work was satisfactory. So in the evenings when the days were long, and on every Saturday, the lad worked with a will in the fields.

On a Saturday in April, Willie was returning with John Matches from peat cutting when they saw a pony and trap drawn up.

'Who can this be?' asked John.

'I just hope it's no the doctor,' murmured Willie.

'It's no him. We'll go in and see.'

Breakfast was ready for them, and already seated were Willie's grandfather and Tomison, both looking older than they had done over two years earlier.

'Willie!' exclaimed Tomison. 'You're growing tall and strong I see. The minister tells me you're doing well with him. Do you still like the learning?'

'Yes, Mr Tomison, but I work more on the farm now.'

'Then you may want to farm, Willie,' said Tomison.

'He works well, but his heart's no in it,' said Mrs Fea. 'Is that no right, Willie?'

'Yes, I have no thought of being a farmer.'

'But he does a man's work and does it well,' added Walter Fea.

'I'm glad to hear that. Mr Peace speaks well of him as a scholar, and will keep on with him for three years at the least. You want to go on with it, Willie?'

'Yes, I want to go on. In winter, there's plenty of time at nights.'

'That's so, and the minister is anxious to have you. I've arranged for the three years.' Then, turning to Walter Fea. 'If there's any hitch, write to me at the Hudson's Bay. It will take time as we can write home only once a year.'

'Hudson's Bay, Mr Tomison!' exclaimed Mrs Fea. 'I thought you had retired for good.'

'No retirement for me, Mrs Fea. I've not been well since coming back to Orkney, and I'm off again in July. Mind you, I'll not be master of all inland again, but will only have my post independent of the officers of the Company out there.'

The three Feas stared at the grizzled old man in amazement.

'It's past belief, Mr Tomison,' said Mrs Fea, 'you goin''

back to that land o' snow and wild beasts, and at your age.'

'It's true I'm sixty-eight, and I'm surprised myself. Only I haven't had health here. My life's lain out there, and I'll battle up the Saskatchewan again, and see the spring ice piled high along its banks, thirty feet of it, and drink it when it melts. A man that once drinks of the Saskatchewan cannot leave it.'

'But, Mr Tomison, you could be dead there for months, and there'd be nobody to give you a Christian burial.'

Tomison gave a grunt.

'There was a man,' he said, 'that gave orders to have his body pickled in a cask of rum and brought back by ship for burial. But for me, if I died here I'd as soon they carried my bones northwest.'

A picture flashed in Willie's mind. The thought came to his grandmother who said, 'Our one boy's bones lie scattered out there, I don't ken where, and I wish wi' all my soul they were in the kirkyard here so I could say a prayer ower them.'

'Aye,' answered Tomison slowly, 'for this has been your dwelling place. Rupert's Land has been mine. And its native folks need God-fearing men there. The Northwest and the Hudson are bitter rivals now, Willie, and both companies are killing them with rum. I wrote to the Governor of the Canadas to stop the trade in it, but he paid no heed.'

'The Indians don't have to take it,' protested Mrs Fea. 'They could clothe their nakedness.'

'Once they've had it,' said Tomison ponderously, 'they'll give furs, wives, bairns, and all for it.'

'Mighty!' exclaimed Walter Fea. 'But we have some like that here.'

'We all have our faults. Some Indians look on liquor as an evil spirit. Aye, I've met fine folks among them. Willie's mother was one of them. A fine, clever woman she was.' The old man paused, looking at the stone floor.

Walter Fea cleared his throat and spoke sadly, more to himself than to the others. 'And I judged her hard. May God forgive me, for she gave us Willie, our comfort now.'

Tomison looked up. 'We won't dwell on that either,' he said gruffly. 'I've made arrangements with the minister to take Willie for three years as I said. But you may need him for work.'

'As long as I have strength, he'll keep with it,' said Walter Fea.

'Well, since you like to learn, Willie, and have time to put to it, you'll keep on for three more years?'

'I will, thank you, sir.'

'Now, I'll away, and will soon be aboard ship back to where I belong. In the good hope of seeing you all again, good-bye.'

The big old man rose with difficulty and went away in the trap. The question he left with Willie, that of his occupation for life, became more pressing with the passing of the days, for plainly his grandfather was failing.

A year and a half had passed after Tomison's departure when one evening Walter Fea did not return. Willie went out and found him dead beside the plough. For a time he could but stare. Then he got John Matches to come with the cart, and they lifted his grandfather's thin body into it. Willie drove the cart, and John unhitched the plough horses, and took them to the stable.

'It'll be hard on thee, Willie. I'll tell her.'

'No, it's my job, John. It will be harder on her.'

Mrs Fea was sitting in her straw-backed chair. She looked sadly at Willie. 'You don't need to tell me, boy. Your face tells me.'

Willie started to sob.

'It's no time to be soft, Willie. Get John to stretch him on a board, and go to Jamie Waas and tell him to come and measure him for the coffin. The funeral will be in three days. John and you will tell the folks.'

Willie did so, and two days later, helped his grand-mother to clothe Walter Fea in his shroud, and lift him into the coffin. His grandmother spoke little. She moved slowly, several times between her chair and her husband. Willie sat silently with her during these days. Then came the funeral. She stood at the door while the men bore her husband to the kirkyard, Willie walking at the head of the coffin. At the kirkyard he helped to lower the box down, and watched it being covered in. He returned to Nether Ardvik in deep sorrow.

His grandmother next day turned to the business of the farm. She and Willie decided to keep it going, Willie to give all his time to it. Mrs Fea, however, declined rapidly, and died in late January, two weeks before Willie's eighteenth birthday. Willie felt, in returning from her burial that he had lost all he had in the world.

He had to dispose of his grandparents' personal effects, which consisted chiefly of the clothes they wore. He gave these to Kitty and to John Matches to dispose of. There was only enough money to pay the funeral expenses and that of a headstone. But there was a little tin deed box, and it was marked *William Fea, Grandson*. In it was a letter from the Hudson's Bay Company which stated that it was sending to Walter Fea the moneys earned by his son which had not been drawn at the time of his death. The money in the box was a guinea and a crown.

Soon Willie found he had indeed lost much. The laird rented the farm to an Aberdeen farmer already established on a small farm in Orkney. When the stock and implements were sold, the law firm gave the proceeds to a distant cousin in another island, for Walter Fea left no will, and there was no record of a grandson. Willie had no proof that he was his father's son. Wondering what he was to do, he went to see Mr Peace.

The minister told him he had no immediate worry, for Tomison had left enough to tutor him for another year, and he could stay at the manse. If he worked on the minister's glebe, the money would last longer, and Mr Peace would try to get him into a writer's office.

9

Another Link Snapped

At Candlemas Willie, having taken his few belongings to
the manse, returned to Nether Ardvik to take the key to
the laird. There he bade farewell to Kitty and John
Matches, who had found employment, and who liked
their new master. He returned to have a look at the house
which had been his home, recalling that eight years ago
he had had his birthday feast there and his first gyro
night adventure. The boys would not have the gyro game
this night; the storm was wild. Willie wandered aimlessly
down to the sea which dashed itself against the cliffs. Its
turbulence soothed him, he felt.

Unaware of where he was going, he bent his steps to
old Nellie's dwelling, sprayed with the spume dashed from
the rocks below. With the roar of the sea in his ears, he
looked down on the boat-roofed hut, thinking of the day
when he and his two friends had been marked by the old
packy woman. In a lull between blasts, he thought he heard
a moan. He listened. In between the crashes of billows
on rocks he heard it again. He ran down the short slope.

'It's me, Nellie, Willie Fea. Are thoo ill?'

'Dyin', boy. Come in,' came a quavering voice. Willie
pulled open the rickety door, and had difficulty in shutting
it.

'The cruizie lamp's opposite thee head on the shelf, and
the steel and flint. Light it.'

The old voice was firmer. Willie groped, found the steel and flint, and lit the rush which floated in fish oil in the blackened lamp. The old woman lay in her rags on a heather couch, her wisps of grey hair straggling down and framing her blue, beak nose, and her ashen, sunken cheeks.

'The sight o' thee maks me better, Willie. Boy, thoo've lost thee folks and thee home. Where does thoo go now?'

'To the minister's in the meantime, but I can't stay there long. I don't ken what I'll do.' Willie's mind was back on himself.

'Thoo'll hae to go back to thee mother's folk, boy, for thee father's are gone. Go wi' Willie Tomison.'

'Among the Indians?'

'Thee mother's folk, aye.'

'Nellie, they told me that you saw the Indians kill my folks, and would have killed me. I'm no goin' near them.'

'Boy, boy, don't go against thee own blood. It will out. I see . . .'

'Thoo sees . . . ?'

'Boy,' quavered the old woman faintly, 'me breath's failin'. Run for the minister. Hasty.'

The woman lay back on her shoulder breathing heavily. Even in the dim light of the old lamp, Willie could see the end was near. He went out, closed the door, and raced through the spume, over the headland, down to the beach, past the school and on to the manse, breaking in on the minister.

'Old Nellie's dyin' and wants you, Mr Peace,' he gasped. 'Hurry.'

'Poor old soul. I'll come directly. Run and tell her, Willie.'

Willie hurried back against the storm. As he neared the school, Hew Rendall hailed him through the gale.

'What's wrong, Willie?' came hollow from the school.

'Old Nellie's dyin'. Mr Peace is comin'.'

'I'll come too. Run on.'

Willie ran on into the wind, and went breathless in through the small door. The cruizie lamp flickered and steadied, and Willie could see the old lips blowing tiny bubbles, and the eyes half-closed. He gazed at her helplessly, and was relieved when Hew Rendall pushed open the door and closed it. The blast of wind seemed to revive Nellie. Her eyes opened.

'Hew Rendall,' she muttered feebly. 'Thoo're a good man.'

The eyes half closed again. The breathing laboured worse for a short time. Suddenly it ceased, and the eyes dropped open just as Mr Peace arrived.

'She just died, sir,' said Willie brokenly.

'Poor body!' mumbled the minister, and bent over Nellie.

When he straightened he said, 'I came as fast as my old legs would carry me, but too late.' He closed the old eyes, and the three stood with bowed heads while he said a prayer.

They went out, shutting the little door, and stood silent on the windswept beach.

At last Hew Rendall shouted above the blast. 'I'll make a box for her, Mr Peace, and will stretch her on a board. None will come to the funeral, I suppose.'

'Not many, I fear, in weather like this, and it will last.'

'I'll get Magnus and Geordie,' said Willie eagerly. 'They'll come.'

c

'Yes,' said Hew. 'You three were marked by her. It is fitting.'

'I'll see that old Johnnie digs the grave,' said the minister. 'We'll bury her on the third day.'

Three days later, through a drenching rain, Hew Rendall, Geordie Merriman, Willie Fea, and Magnus Isbister, a pole between each pair, carried the rough box with the dried-up body of Old Nellie the packy woman from her boat dwelling along the beach to the kirkyard, Mr Peace following. After she had been lowered in, Mr Peace prayed, and again after the grave was filled in. The six men then stood silent. Finally old Johnnie, the grave digger, who had seen many burials, said, 'Old Nellie will be a proud woman this day. Mr Rendall and three young men carryin' her here, and Mr Peace prayin' ower her. She had few friends, and if she had chosen, she would have picked out the five o' you.'

They separated, Willie going with the minister, who was silent. Willie, feeling strange in going to his new home, wished he would speak, but realised that Mr Peace would be thinking of Nellie. Yet he felt even more rootless. Old Nellie in some strange way had been a link between his grandparents and his father and himself. She could see before and after. There were no links now to his father's people. He knew of none to his mother's people, and in spite of what Nellie had said to him when she was dying, he was determined there would be none.

10

Resistance

The days following old Nellie's funeral continued wet and
stormy. Rain and spray driven by the wind against the
cottages of Ardvik had lifted the thatches of some and so
saturated others that there were continuous drops and
trickles running to the earthen floors. The dripping water
mixing with the soot from the open peat fires blackened
the low walls and turned the floors into dirty mud. Until
the rain and wind abated, the cottars had to suffer dis-
comfort and dampness. They looked forward to Sunday
when they expected the minister to do something about it.

The kirk was comparatively clean when they gathered
on Sunday. Willie and Geordie sat with the Isbisters,
Willie now with no folks of his own, and Geordie coming
from a neighbouring parish.

It was the custom for the precenter, Hew Rendall, to
remind the minister for what and for whom to pray after
the sermon and the closing psalm. Like other teachers
and ministers, both Hew Rendall and Mr Peace prided
themselves on making simple verse quite extemporary, and
occasionally did so in the very last prayer. As a con-
sequence, the congregation always looked forward to this
prayer with some interest, and listened more carefully
than they did to the ordinary prayer.

They were not disappointed on this day. At the close
of the psalm, Hew sonorously recited in a chant:

For the rain to stop
And the wind to cease,
For the soul of old Nellie,
Pray, Mr Peace.

The people, waiting a little longer for the prayer than they did when there was no verse, knew they were to get a rhyme. The prayer came soon, however, and Mr Peace chanted:

Oh Thou who makest all things whole
Take to Thee Nellie Howland's soul.
And, as Thou did'st on Galilee,
Stop the wind and still the sea.

As the service ended, a beam of sunlight glinted through the tiny window, and the people realised that the roar of the wind had died down. The smell of damp clothes went out of the little kirk with them, a smell like that of the wet sheep on which the serges and twills had grown from two to twenty years earlier. As each person came out, he glanced at the sky, and bowed his head. Then the people gathered in little groups according to the directions in which their homes lay.

Willie, Geordie, and Magnus stood a little apart as Mr and Mrs Isbister conversed with others, and listened to the conversation.

'Faith that was a powerful prayer, Tammie,' said Mathew Sabiston in his high-pitched voice.

'Aye, and the Lord has answered,' Tammie solemnly replied.

'Willie and Geordie, ye'll come home wi' Mansie and have a bite wi' us,' invited Mrs Isbister.

'Aye, and thanks, Mrs Isbister,' answered Geordie.

'Any word from the boys, Mary?' asked Mrs Louttit.

'None for a while, Babbie. Young Tammie's ship will be ower in America lookin' after the sugar ships, and Robbie's wi' Collingwood in the Mediterranean.'

'So we think, wife, so we think,' amended Tam Isbister. 'We have no word for months, and they might be at the bottom o' the sea for a' we ken.'

'Poor boys,' Mrs Louttit commiserated. 'Both o' them forced into the navy by the lairds and leavin' thee only Mansie, and both in Trafalgar four months ago.'

'They both say that the endless watchin' and never gettin' a night's sleep is worse than Trafalgar,' Tam Isbister remarked.

'Mebbe,' said his wife shortly, 'but it's glàd I am that they're no gettin' their heads blawn off every minute. Some day I hope the good Lord will put an end to the war.'

Willie felt that this was not his world. He had no brothers to be in this war that seemed an unreal thing. Now with his grandparents gone, how little he had to share with those in this parish in which he had lived most of his life. He was glad to see Hew Rendall and Mr Peace approach, for with them he shared some things the others did not share.

'Willie,' said Mr Peace, 'I must over the hill to christen a bairn. You'll have to starve till I get back.'

'He and Geordie's comin' wi' us, Mr Peace.'

'That's grand. Willie needs company. I must hurry. God be with you all.' And the minister turned away.

'Mr Rendall, will you no come and hae a bite wi' us, too, such as it is?' invited Mrs Isbister.

'Gladly, thank you. You'll be going by the road.'

'Aye, Mr Rendall,' said Tam Isbister, 'it's the short

way for me, and me rheumaties don't make walkin' a pleasure any more.'

The four friends set off by the shore, past old Nellie's empty dwelling, on which they looked down in silence for a few minutes. Then Magnus and Geordie went in front, and Willie and Hew Rendall dropped behind. With the others out of earshot, Hew Rendall asked, 'Any prospects of a career yet, Willie?'

'Not much, Mr Rendall. I think Mr Peace is getting me in a writer's office in Kirkwall. It will do as well as another, I suppose.'

'You are not keen on it?'

'Not very, but I must do something soon.'

'Did Mr Tomison, when he called, hold out no prospect?'

'He said he would get me into the Hudson's Bay Company, but I'll do anything before that, even go to the army.'

'I see. You are missing a fine opportunity.'

'I can't help it.'

'I think I understand. Yet you are by birth and character one who would understand Indians, and be trusted by them, from what I hear. Since that way is closed, you will have to think carefully whether you want to be a writer. Your education gives you a chance to choose. Remember, I'll give you a recommendation when you need it.'

'Thank you, Mr Rendall.'

Magnus and Geordie were waiting for them, and no more was said. During the meal, Willie was very quiet, and remained silent all evening. As he was never talkative and as he had had a great loss, the others did not think much about it until Hew Rendall rose to go. His way home and Willie's way to the manse were one way, but Willie lingered quietly on, and left only after Hew would be home.

When he did leave, he walked back to the manse tight-lipped. Tomison, old Nellie, and now Hew Rendall urging him to go to Rupert's Land where his parents' bones lay scattered! They had all hinted it was his duty, so it seemed to him. Why? He had no duty there, and he would not go.

II

Press Gang Busy

On his twenty-first birthday, Willie, serving his third year as a clerk with Mr Firth in Kirkwall, had a few days' holiday, and decided to walk to Ardvik. When he started out from his lodgings, the morning was bright and sunny, promising a week or two of the good weather that occasionally came in February. He walked with a long easy stride, his black eyes sweeping from the hill to the road, from the road to the sea where a frigate tacked its way through a channel between two small islands, and a navy cutter was overhauling a small boat.

'Some poor fisher boy about to be pressed into the navy,' he thought. The naval press gangs were again active on the coast, seizing every serviceable man they could lay hands on with no regard to the law stating that only those men selected by lot from the lists supplied by town or parish council were to be forced in to the army or navy. No doubt the naval press gangs were confident that any young man who had not already been picked for service would be immediately they seized him. The naval cutters and the land constables had gathered in almost every able-bodied man up to 1806, but after Trafalgar, they had been inactive for three years. Now in 1810 they were very active. Few young men escaped them, and the rumour was that they were already taking older ones.

The occasional woman at a roadside cottage eyed

Willie's long, lean form as he swung along, probably watching carefully to give warning if a press gang was on the move, for all helped men to escape except the councils and their constables. The road was empty before him until he came to the village of Finstown. There he made his way to the ale house, for he was warm through walking in his long coat, heavy breeches, and thick stockings.

As he drew near, a well-built young man limped from the ale house, stood lifting his foot for a minute by the door, limped a few steps one way, and then back to the door. He seemed in pain, and Willie hurried in order to help him. The man limped away again, turned his head, looked all around, and then dashed off at a fast run. As Willie gazed after him in astonishment, two men ran from the door, and gazed wildly around.

'There he goes,' shouted one, pointing to the man who was taking the hill at a great pace.

'Here's your staff; after him!' yelled the other, and both set off in pursuit.

The stout ale-house keeper ambled from the door, and looked after the running men. 'Hee, hee, hee!' he wheezed.

'What is happening?' demanded Willie.

'Oh, what a deceitfu' villain is that young man. He made the poor constables believe – hee, hee, – that his ankle was broken. They – hee, hee – let him go to the door to exercise it before starting for Kirkwall. Now, they'll go there and tell that the man can't be found. It's very wicked o' the lad. Hee, hee. You'll be needin' a drink o' ale this warm day. Hee, hee, hee!'

'You don't think they'll catch him?'

'Hee, hee. He's no fool, that lad. But it was wicked o' him after the king's staff had been laid on his shoulder.'

Willie drank his ale in silence, the host sitting near with his hands across his stomach, silent also except for an occasional hee, hee. Willie paid for his ale, and took the road that wound through rugged hills, and in the afternoon, Ardvik came in view. He reached Gairstone Cottage, and called in.

'Willie Fea!' exclaimed Mrs Isbister. 'My, I'm blithe to see thee. And are thoo likin' the office work?'

'Not well, Mrs Isbister, but it's all right, and Mr Firth is kind.'

'Thoo does no like it. Willie, thoo should have gone wi' Mr Tomison.'

'Maybe I should, Mrs Isbister, but it's too late to change. Is Magnus near at hand?'

'Mansie? Aye, he's up at the quarry under the Fiold Hill, gettin' stones for the wall, he's biggin' roond the laird's hoose. Geordie Merriman is helpin' him for a day or two, quarryin' and cartin' the stones. Thoo'll find both there.'

'Thanks, Mrs Isbister, and I'll be in to see you and Tom before I go back.'

Willie turned off the road into a cart track that led to the green mounds of grass and the piles of clay that marked the stone quarry. A heap of blue stones, all with at least one straight edge, lay on the edge of a hole about seven feet deep and twenty yards square. Down on the rock strata, Magnus, maul in hand, bent over a large slab which Geordie was levering with a heavy crowbar. Willie hailed them.

'Willie,' they both shouted, and dropped their tools. As they came up, Willie noted that Magnus had grown some, but he was still short, slim, and wiry. Geordie, however, was now on the big side, broad-shouldered and fleshy. Geordie's hair had changed from light to dark brown; that of Magnus was still white.

'On holiday, Willie?' asked Magnus.

'A few days off, and I came to see the old place.'

'Did thoo walk all the way, Willie?' asked Geordie. 'Thee legs will be stiff.'

'No, I enjoyed the walk, and did not hurry. It took me five hours.'

'Nothing new on the road, I suppose?' asked Magnus.

'Yes, there was. At Finstown a man escaped the constables who were taking him to Kirkwall. He had convinced them that he had broken his ankle, and limped about while they were in the ale-house. Just as I came up, he took off up the hill like a hare. By the time the constables started after him, he was going over the ridge. The ale-house keeper was amused.'

'They would be the press gang constables takin' the man to Kirkwall to be examined by the doctor,' remarked Geordie. 'The doctor says if they're fit for the navy or army.'

'That's one they won't get – no just yet,' murmured Magnus.

'Aye, and it's one more that must go,' sighed Geordie. 'They'll come for me any day now.'

'For you? Why do you think so?'

'There's only three young men left near me home, and one's the son o' the laird and the other o' a factor. That leaves me. No laird will pay out forty pounds if he can name some poor body.'

'Forty pounds? How is this, Magnus?'

'Well, Willie, the parish has to get so many men for the service. If it doesn't, the landholders have to pay forty pounds for each man it can't raise. In this parish the laird at North Skaill and Mr Heddle o' South Skaill, that's him I'm workin' for, would have to pay. In some places where there's no lairds it's the big farmers who have men workin' for them. They have the power to draw up the lists o' young men and hand them to the constables who arrest them.'

'I thought the naval press gangs did that work.'

'Aye they do, on the sea, searchin' every boat on it, for if there's a young fellow aboard he'll either be named already or they'll get him named.'

'I see. Geordie could have his name given then.'

'Aye, I could, and that easy,' said Geordie gloomily. 'Only three o' me age in the parish and two will no be named.'

'There was no talk of this when I was here,' said Willie.

'No, for they did no need men after Trafalgar,' explained Magnus. 'But now, wi' John Moore and his men killed at Corunna and wi' them landing a new army in Portugal that will have more killed, they'll want men.'

'What about you, Magnus?'

'Safe, I think. I'm workin' for the laird, and he'll see I'm no on the list, for I have two brothers in the Navy already. It's the law that they don't tak' the last son.'

'Ach,' said Geordie in disgust, 'they never keep the law. If that Harold Heddle was old enough his name would no go down.'

'Harold Heddle, the laird's son,' mused Willie. 'He was just beginning with Mr Peace when I went to Kirkwall. The minister had a job tutoring him until he used the strap. I don't think the laird liked it.'

'He's wi' me every day when I'm working on the wall,' said Magnus. 'First he got in the way all the time, and burned his boots and stockings in the lime I was slaking.

Now, he tries to help. But thoo're wrong, Geordie. If Harold was old enough, he would have his name in the list just to go against his father. Are thoo here for the week-end?'

'Yes,' answered Willie.

'I'll tell thee what, Geordie. Willie and I will come to thee on Saturday night and make a hidy-hole for thee. Thoo'll come, Willie?'

'Gladly. I want to see what you make.'

'Look for us, then, Geordie, after day set.'

'Aye, I will,' said Geordie, readily. 'I'm no just itching to be mixed up wi' these blood-thirsty Frenchmen.'

'And I'll be now on my way to the manse,' said Willie, and turned to go.

12

The Hiding Place

'Geordie is not likely to make a soldier or sailor,' remarked Willie, while he and Magnus were tramping over the heather as the sun sank on Saturday.

'No,' answered Magnus slowly. 'Geordie thinks only about farming. He works well enough wi' me in the quarry, but he does no like it. Me, now, I like workin' wi' stones, blue in the heart and straight on the edge. But I like other things, fishing and sailing, and I don't dislike turnin' my hand to help my folks wi' the croft.'

'I wish I could get interested in these things,' said Willie.

'But you're a writer, above that sort o' work. Clerks don't dirty their hands except wi' ink.'

'Yet I'm restless, Mansie. I feel out of my place and time.'

'Boy, you've been here all my life, it seems.' Magnus turned and they both looked down the hill. Ardvik lay in shadows, but the straits were pink and motionless, framed with the hills of Hrossey, but streaming dark red between it and Spear. 'Look,' Magnus continued, 'the three of us went to Hew Rendall doon there, and it was there we got marked by Old Nellie. And there we had our gyro fire. But that was before your grandfolks died.'

'Yes,' said Willie, sadly. 'Before they died. Since then I'm like a bit of driftwood. Oh, Mansie, you and Geordie have been my friends, and the folks here kind, especially Mr Peace and Hew Rendall. But I'm restless.'

'You're still queer, Willie. Settled in better work than stone or the ground, and yet you sheer from it as you did from the reek o' the fire.'

The two turned and walked again up the hill. The smoke of the fire. Willie had felt a sort of turning within him as the vision of a smoking ruin with dead bodies flashed into his mind. For a moment he looked on a woman lying face down, the back of her head bloody. His mother. The half of him. He forced the vision away as the two reached the crest of the hill and looked down on Geordie's home. All these years Willie had never before visited it.

The Meriman croft, twenty acres on the slope of another hill, had been carved out of the surrounding moorland. The farmstead was enclosed by a dry stone dyke, and stood on the high bank of a burn. The low house was flagstoned, but the attached barn and byre were thatched. A stable stood apart from the barn. Behind the cottage were two peat stacks, and, nearer the barn, five small grain stacks. An open view lay all around so that in daylight no one could approach unseen. And Geordie could not leave unseen by a watcher. His refuge had to be inside the stone dyke and within the yard, Magnus decided, as the two approached.

While Willie was speaking to the Merrimans, Magnus went round the buildings. Geordie's nook bed in the ben-end of the cottage jutted out beyond the eaves just next the peat stacks, and it was roofed by two flagstones. Magnus noted that the grain stacks obscured the view from one side. He came to the others.

'I'm goin' to make these two stones slide over one another so that Geordie can get out from inside. Now, you two must clear a hole in the peat stack, two feet square for Geordie to crawl in, and bigger inside so he can lie without gettin' the cramps.'

'Bless me, Mansie,' said Robbie Merriman, 'anybody could see the hole and pry into it.'

'Aye, so the entrance must be built up with one layer of peats, and it'll never show,' said Mansie. 'I think we'll come in the morning, for it's darkenin' now.'

'We're no workin' here on the Sabbath Day,' declared Robbie Merriman.

'But, Mr Merriman,' expostulated Willie, 'it's to save Geordie.'

'Mebbe,' replied Robbie, 'but Mr Peace will no like it, wi' thee in it too.'

'Robbie,' said Magnus, 'if thee ox or thee ass goes in the ditch on Sunday, thoo does no wait till Monday to take him out.'

'No, and if me ox or me ass, which I don't have, went into the ditch on a Saturday night, I'm no waitin' to Sunday mornin' to take him out neither. We'll finish this night. I'll get two lanthorns.'

Mansie was nettled, but he said 'All right, Robbie, but thoo'll have to help me wi' the flagstones, and Mrs Merriman will take the peat from the boys.'

'I'll do that gladly,' said Mrs Merriman, anxious about her one son. 'I'll get the cubbies to carry them in.' She went to the barn and returned with two straw baskets called cubbies.

After toiling in the dark for over an hour, Mansie managed to arrange the flagstones so that they slid easily over one another. He had been particularly careful, and had enjoyed making Robbie Merriman hold up a flagstone for longer than was needed. Then both went to the peat stack, and saw in the darkness that Geordie was placing the peats covering the opening into position, and Willie was tossing the peats they had taken out of the centre of the stack into a cubby.

'We've made an arched room inside,' said Willie.

Mansie stooped down and pushed the covering peats inside, then he crawled in, and replaced them behind him.

'Does that look all right?'

His voice sounded hollow to those outside. 'Nobody would ken thoo're in there,' replied Robbie Merriman, holding the lanthorn to the closed entrance.

Mansie crawled out, replaced the peats, and said 'Noo, Geordie, into the house wi' thee, and see how quiet thoo can get out and in here.'

Geordie went in, and soon his head appeared in the lanthorn's beam. He wriggled awkwardly on to the eaves for some time, dropped to the ground, and hunkered across to the stack. He crawled in and replaced the peats for the entrance. Mansie examined the stack.

'Come out, Geordie, and mind to cover the hole,' he said.

Geordie came out. 'Come out o' the nook feet first, Geordie, and thoo're ready to drop.'

'But when will I ken it's safe to come out o' this hole. They might be watchin' the house.'

'Thee folks will have to tell thee. They'll come out and look aroond, and say, "Where can that boy o' ours have got to?"'

'But,' objected Robbie, 'they might still be around.'

'Well, keep on speakin', and while you two speak, Geordie can go in and go to bed.'

'Well, it might work,' said Geordie.

'Well, Willie, let's away home,' said Magnus.

'You'll both have a drink o' the wife's ale afore you go,' Robbie Merriman said.

'No, Robbie, for the Sabbath Day will fall on us drinkin' ale,' said Magnus.

'Mansie, that's very stickit o' thee,' grumbled Robbie.

'It is that,' said Willie. 'Come, Mansie, we'll drink Robbie's health.'

Mansie laughed, pleased he had scored off Robbie Merriman. When Willie and he took their way back to Ardvik, Willie said, 'If that's what a man must do to escape, I'd sooner go.'

'But, Willie, what's the use o' beatin' the French if we can't beat the lairds?' asked Magnus. 'This naming everybody but their own! We must escape if we can.'

13

The Aff-hand Lad

Another year had almost gone by, and as another Candle-mas drew near, Willie asked for and received a few days holiday. He made the journey to Ardvik, and was welcomed by the minister and his wife. He spent much of his time, however, with Magnus who was still building the wall round South Skaill. He helped to mix mortar, fill in the centre with rock chips, and pick out suitable stones for Magnus. Harold Heddle, the laird's son, was there every day, a sturdy lad of ten, short, upturned nose, and pale face. The first day Willie appeared, Harold eyed him up and down and sideways, moving his head quickly like a cormorant, and said, 'I saw thee at the minister's when I started there.'

'Yes, I remember. Why are you not there today?'

'I've got better to do, that's why. Thoo'll no be o' much help here, comin' from the town.'

'I'll learn, Harold,' said Willie, and began mixing some sand and lime.

The boy watched him keenly. 'Thoo has too little lime in that, Willie. It'll never hold a stone. Mansie puts more in.'

'Does he, Harold? Well, I'll add a little.'

Willie shovelled in a little more, mixed the whole, still dry, and then shaped the mixture into a ring. He began pouring water from a bucket into the ring.

'That's plenty, Willie. Look, boy, it's runnin' out.'

'Ah, but we'll be clever and catch it,' said Willie, scooping up the overflow. Then he began scraping the dry outside into the wet centre, and after going all round, he mixed the whole until it was evenly damp and soft. Unused to the work, he leaned for a minute on his shovel.

'Mansie mixes it more than that,' said the boy. 'I doubt it will no hold.'

Willie looked at him. 'You should use your handkerchief, Harold. The lime will get into your lungs.'

The boy seized his nose between thumb and finger, blew, and snapped the bubbles towards Willie. They fell short, and Harold pulled out his handkerchief and wiped his nose.

'That's no right mixed, Mansie,' he said, pointing to the mortar.

Magnus winked to Willie, came over, and shovelled the mortar a little.

'It's well mixed, Harold. Thoo're just being awkward.'

Sulkily the boy turned from them and busied himself with turning over stones. As Mansie resumed building and Willie filled a bucket with mortar, the laird came down from his house, a walking stick in his hand. He was a short, stout man, red-faced, wearing a brown serge suit with a cravat round his neck.

'Harold, lad, don't do that,' he said gently.

The boy did not look at him. He lifted a stone, staggered, and dropped it, jumping clear as it fell.

'Harold, you'll break a leg.'

Harold paid no heed to his father, but lifted another stone.

'Harold,' said the laird sharply, 'stop it.'

The boy rubbed the stone up and down his stomach.

'Stop that, boy. You're spoiling your clothes.'

'That's just the stone I need here, Harold,' Mansie broke in. 'Give it to me.'

The boy handed the stone to Magnus, and watched him while he fitted it into the wall. The laird went in front, squinted down first one side of the wall and then the other.

'A good bit of stone work, Magnus, my man,' he said, and moved off, saying, 'Send that boy home if he gets in your way.'

Magnus resumed building, and Willie picked out suitable stones for him. Harold moved up to the front where his father had stood, jerked his head forward to glance down one side, jerked it sideways to glance at the other, and said in a rumbling voice, 'A good bit of stone work that, my man. Send Willie home if he gets in your way.'

Both the young men bent over their work, trying hard to keep from laughing. After a while Magnus said, 'Thoo'll go home, now, Harold, as thee father said.'

Harold paid no attention. Magnus and Willie worked on in silence, Magnus taking the stones Harold offered but throwing them down as unsuitable. After accepting one from Willie, Magnus fitted it in and turned to Willie while he held the stone in position, his thumb marking the spot where he wanted it broken.

'Hand me the hammer, Willie.'

Harold seized the hammer and held it out. Magnus paid no heed to him, but stood looking at the pile of stones.

'I'll have that one next, Will . . .' and Magnus let out a yell. Harold had brought the mason hammer down on his thumbnail. Magnus thrust his thumb in his mouth, pulled it out, and yelled, 'Get home, boy.' Harold turned his back, and busied himself among the stones. Magnus seized him, sat down on the pile, laid Harold across his knee, and gave him six quick slaps with his open hand. The boy made no sound. When Magnus released him he turned and walked slowly homeward. He turned again and glared at Magnus.

'Mansie Isbister,' he shrilled, 'I'll be even wi' thee yet. Just wait till I'm master here.'

He glared at Mansie a full minute, and stalked off home.

'Quite a lad,' said Willie, amused at the incident.

'Aye, he's an aff-hand lad as my father keeps telling him. He'll be back when he gets over his temper.'

'Has he come here every day since you started?'

'No, he goes to the minister's most o' the time, but if he feels like no goin', he comes here.'

'Does his father have no control over him?'

'I never saw Harold pay the slightest heed to the laird. The first boy died, and they've spoiled this one, both him and his wife.'

'Quite a plucky lad. You used a heavy hand on him.'

'I've never heard him greet for pain. I should no have thrashed him, for he might no have meant to hit my thumb,' said Magnus. 'It's no comfortable,' he added, looking at the nail, turning from blue to black.

'Here's the laird coming back. He might have seen you.'

'I'll tell him anyway, even if it costs me the job.'

'Surely no,' murmured Willie as the laird drew near.

'Harold's not here,' said the laird genially. 'He obeyed me for once.'

Both his hearers were silent for a minute; then Magnus held out his thumb. 'You see that, Mr Heddle. Harold hit me wi' the mason hammer.'

The laird gave a loud laugh. 'Just like the boy,' he said.

'I laid him across my knee and gave him a few clouts.' Magnus looked steadily at the laird, who turned purple.

'You hit my son,' he spluttered.

'Aye, after he hit me thumb. And you told me to make him go home.'

The laird was silent for a minute. 'Isbister,' he said quietly, 'I've never lifted a hand against him, and I'm not having others do it.'

He shook his stick with the royal coat of arms engraved on it at Magnus, turned, and strode away home.

The two watched him in silence. When he disappeared inside, Willie asked, 'Do you lose your job now?'

'He did shake his constable's staff at me, but he'll call to mind I have two brothers serving. He would have told me now if I had lost the job. He'll get over it.'

'Even if Harold complains?'

'I don't think Harold will. He'd scream at the laird if he thought I was no building more wall. He'll be here in the morning.'

When the sun was well in the west, the two stopped for the day, and went to Gairstone Cottage, the home of the Isbisters.

14

Escape

'Come awa' in, Willie,' greeted Mrs Isbister, ushering him into the little kitchen where her husband sat by the fire in a straw-backed chair.

'Is the writing grand?' asked Tam Isbister.

'There's nothing grand about a clerk's life, I assure you.'

'Boy, Willie, thoo speaks now like the gentry, and no like the Ardvik folk,' Tam Isbister said.

'Yes, I must not use *thoo* and *thee*, I'm told.'

'Thoo'll think little o' the stone work,' Tam continued. 'It's no like handlin' books and sheets o' paper.'

'It's a change. Handling sheets of paper is tedious work. We've had an interesting day with the laird's son and the laird himself.'

'Aye, Harold. He's an aff-hand lad if there ever was one, and that's what I've said for years. What was he up to?'

'He was in to everything, and ended up by hitting Magnus on the thumb with the hammer.'

'The imp o' Satan. Yet one can't help likin' him.'

'Yes, I was quite taken with him though he thinks me stupid. But he did not take well to the thrashing Magnus gave him.'

'Did thoo thrash him, Magnus? The laird will no like that,' said Mrs Isbister.'

'I did no give him much, Mother, and I'll be losin' my thumbnail. I told the laird about it, and he was no pleased; said the boy was not to be touched.'

'Thoo'll lose thee job, I doubt,' said Tam.

'I don't think I'll hear more about it. He does no keep his temper up for long.'

After supper Willie said, 'The press gangs seem active again. How is Geordie faring? I'm glad I don't have to run from the lairds' men.'

'No, Willie, it's no them thoo're runnin' from,' said Mrs Isbister.

Willie looked hard at her, but the old woman gazed at the fire in absent-minded fashion. 'What about Geordie?' he asked again.

'He sticks close to home, and even wears his mother's clothes at times when he's workin' in the field,' laughed Magnus.

'It's no a thing to laugh at, Mansie,' admonished his father. 'Thoo had better to be ready to hide now the laird's in a temper.'

'Father, the laird's no the man to agree to my name goin' to the constables when my two brothers are serving. He's no unfair.'

'Put not your faith in princes,' quoted Tam Isbister. 'He let our two older boys be named, and never warned us.'

'I doubt he could no help it,' said Mrs Merriman. 'Mr Heddle is a kind man, Tam, as thoo kens well.'

'Aye, and he'll let Mansie be named too,' muttered Tam.

The door grated open, and the ten-year-old son of the laird burst in from the darkness outside, all breathless.

'Mansie, Mansie,' he gasped, blinking in the candle-light.

'Mighty, Harold, thoo're come to see me after I gave thee the thrashing for hittin' me thumb wi' the mason's hammer.'

'Mansie, I ...'

'Harold, boy, does thee folks ken thoo're out at this time o' night?' demanded Mrs Isbister.

'Let me speak,' gasped the boy. 'Mansie, the constables are comin' for thee, and will be on the way any time now.'

'This is one o' thee tricks, Harold.'

'I tell thee I heard them say it,' shrilled the boy, 'and I came runnin' to tell thee.'

'Thoo're an aff-hand lad if ever there was one,' said Tam Isbister. 'Who named Mansie?'

'The peerie lairds Charlie Bews and Tam Flett, and Peter Johnson, the son o' the big farmer, and me old fool o' a father.'

'Peter Johnson,' muttered Tam Isbister, 'takes care he does no go.'

'That he does, but me father has to get a man off his land or pay forty pounds.'

'I thought he was my friend,' said Magnus.

'Aye, and so is forty pounds,' said the aff-hand lad.

'They're comin' soon, Harold?' asked Magnus.

'Aye, they were goin' for the lanthorns, and for a horse when I left.'

'Mansie, it's the hills for thee, boy, and quick,' said his mother tearfully.

'Aye, Mother, and I'm glad I had my supper.'

Tam Isbister had been looking through the small window. 'Mansie, thoo must awa'. A light came out from South Skaill. Harold, awa' home or thoo'll be in trouble.'

Mansie had glanced through the window. 'Another lanthorn,' he said, 'and near, I'll awa'.'

'Wait,' broke in Willie. 'Put out the candle. Harold, go out, and when they get near, whistle. I'll run out, and when you hear me, Harold, shout "there he is". I'll run, and they'll follow.'

'Thinkin' thoo're Mansie. Boy, Willie, thoo're fly.'
Harold went out.

'It might work,' whispered Mansie.

'Why not? They don't know I'm here, and I would not
run from them anyway.'

'True, Willie,' said Mrs Isbister, 'it's no them thoo're
runnin' from. Hark!'

A shrill whistle sounded. Harold was evidently using
his fingers to whistle on.

Willie crashed the wooden door open and ran out.

'There he is. There he is!' Harold screamed.

Two forms rose between Willie and the hills. He swung
seaward. Running strongly, he left the pounding feet of
his pursuers behind, but he stumbled on a hole and fell
heavily on his side. Winded by the fall, he rose and listened.
To the left, between him and the hills, he heard a horse's
hooves thud. He angled right, running easily, caring only
to keep his pursuers following, but he stopped suddenly.
The noise of the breaking of waves had stopped him. He
had almost run over the cliff.

Realising now that he was on a narrow headland with
the sea twenty feet below, and that he could be hemmed
in, he turned landward, running fast. Three forms loomed
up, one to his left, one to his right, and one in front. He
feinted left and swerved right, and two forms closed in.
He shot between them, and heard them crash together.
There was a grunt, then a scream, and he sped on. Soon
he came to the rutted road.

There was no noise of the horse again. Willie thought
it best to walk back lest the constables return to the
cottage. Listening intently and hearing nothing, he walked
carefully along. The sound of the horse came from behind.
He flattened himself by the road, and it trotted past.

Listening again, he knew it had turned up the road to South Skaill. He followed slowly, listening and watching, He saw the lights of the lanthorns return to South Skaill, and stood still for a while. Nothing was to be heard or seen. He went slowly to Gairstone.

There was no light in the cottage. Willie knocked gently. 'It's Willie,' he said in a low voice.

'Is it all safe now?' whispered Magnus.

'All seems clear. Two of them crashed together heavily on the headland, and by their yells must have hurt one another.'

'I hope they did,' said Mrs Isbister, 'and are in their beds now. But they'll be back. There'll be no end to it.'

A silence followed. At last, Tam Isbister spoke.

'Mansie, boy, go to Stromness and see if thoo can get on a ship. There's no peace for thee here now.'

'But I ken nobody in Stromness.'

'I'll come with you, Magnus,' said Willie, 'and we'll go to John Stockan, some cousin of my grandfather. He always wanted me to come to see him.'

'The very thing, bless thee, Willie. Awa' the both o' you,' said Mrs Isbister, 'afore the constables come back here.'

As the two young men went, Tam Isbister hummed a version of Psalm one hundred and twenty-four:

> *Even as a bird out of the fowler's snare*
> *Escapes away, so is our soul set free.*
> *Broke are their nets . . .*

'I hope so. Good-bye,' said Willie, as they left the old couple by themselves, no son at home.

The two friends set their stride to the dark and sombre hill and whatever lay beyond for them.

15

Willie Haunted

After Willie and Magnus got over the ridge of the hill, they felt safe, and, tired with their exertions, walked slowly, thinking over their night's excitement.

'Harold is a strange lad, Mansie.'

'Aye, as father said, he's aff-hand.'

'Will he get into trouble over this?'

'Little he cares. His father spoils him, and he does what he likes.'

After a little while Willie asked, 'Will whalers be taking on men now?'

'No likely, but I might get a chance on some ship. I must lie low till the laird's paid his forty pounds.'

'It won't be pleasant to return to Ardvik.'

'Aye, and that's what's botherin' me.'

No more was said for a time. Then Willie spoke slowly. 'There's something bothering me, Mansie. Your mother said that it was not the press gang I'm running from. What did she mean?'

'Ach, Mother says things queerly. She meant that it was not you that was runnin' from them.'

'I don't know. She mentioned before that I should have gone to the Bay. Anyway, I have been running from my mother's people and the land where I was born and where my parents' bones lie scattered.'

'Runnin'! You have no been runnin'.'

'But I have, and Mr Tomison, old Nellie, and Hew Rendall hinted as much. I thought of this first when Mr Tomison said he would as soon his bones lay by the Saskatchewan. Something within drives me, and I can deny it no longer.'

'Boy, Willie, I don't ken what's botherin' you.'

'Magnus, ever since I lost my grandparents I've felt a stranger here, as little as I want to leave. My life lies in the Northwest. You've heard of Lord Selkirk?'

'Him that has the agent in Stromness signin' labourers for his settlement?'

'Yes. I'm going to sign.'

'Mighty boy, wi' your education! Tomison could make thee an officer in the Hudson's Bay.'

'I may see what chances are to be taken as a clerk, but I'll sign as a labourer.'

'Boy, so will I. There'll be no peace in Ardvik for me now.'

As the first glimmer of dawn came over the hill and sent a shaft glittering over the large lake ahead of them, the two friends stopped and shook hands. Then they trudged on along the north side where two swans sailed peering into the reeds as the fresh light of the spring morning spread over the water. They came to the track over the moor on which Willie had first come to Ardvik as a child, and followed it until they stood above the little town of Stromness spread out along the shore, its chimneys one by one sending out spirals of smoke. Over the bright waters beyond, a cloud bank slowly rolled in from Scapa Flow and blurred the town. The two came to John Stockan's house.

'What would you two young men be wantin' early in the day?' asked John Stockan, his grey eyes peering at them from his pale face.

'Mr Stockan, I'm Willie Fea.'

John peered more closely. 'By me faith, boy, so you are. I must be dottin' for you're the grandfather all ower again when he was young. Come in. Wife, here's Willie Fea and a friend.'

'Willie. Deed and it is,' exclaimed Mrs Stockan. 'Boy, we're the only kin you have left. You should have come here when your folks died.'

'Well, I've come now, and for a favour. Mansie here is being pressed, and must keep out of Ardvik for a time.'

'He's welcome here. Why were they pressin' him wi' his two brothers away?'

'That did no help me,' said Mansie.

'It's terrible times for young and old,' said John. 'The young taken, and the old no fit to do the work.'

'John, we're thinking of signing with the agent for Lord Selkirk.'

'Well, that seems a good chance. Plenty o' land free. But you both read and write, Willie. They'll put you to the Company, for they sign the men for both.'

'Where do we find the agent?'

'Captain Spence. I'll take ye to him after breakfast. The two o' you'll be right hungry.'

During breakfast, Magnus told the Stockans of the night's adventures.

'That was well done, Willie. I hope the two constables dunted their heads hard. Now, we'll go up to the agent.'

Captain Spence was a big man with a weather-beaten face, wearing a captain's uniform. The two young men gave their names and made their request known.

'Fea? Son of the Fea killed at South Branch House?'

'Yes, sir.'

'But Mr Tomison spoke of you as for the Company. He said you were getting a good education.'

'Yes, I studied with Mr Peace, the minister, for three years, and I'm now with a writer.'

'You should be engaged as a clerk, not as a labourer.'

'What you see fit, sir, but I wish to be engaged now.'

'I cannot engage you as a clerk now, but Mr Auld at York Factory may, though he and Mr Tomison are not friends. You both want to engage as labourers, then?'

'Will this keep the press gang off me?' asked Magnus.

'They won't take our signed men, Isbister. Here are the contracts. Read them over and see the terms.'

'Well, boys, I'll be lookin' for you,' said Stockan, and left.

Willie and Mansie went over the contracts carefully, Willie reading each item to Mansie. They went over them a second time.

'This seems all right, Magnus.'

'It seems good, and we sign for three years, and get passage home if we want.'

'Yes, Magnus, you can get passage home. I am going to sign.'

'So am I. We're ready, Captain Spence.'

'Good lads. Sign here, then.'

When he had witnessed their signatures, the captain said, 'It will be late in June before the ships sail. Make sure you're here when they come. Meanwhile, there will be no need to worry over the press gang.'

Dull now that their adventure meant waiting, the two young men wandered through the town, and along the shore, wondering at the fact that they met and passed twice as many women as men. When they returned to the Stockan home, they mentioned this.

'Aye,' said John, 'wi' men goin' to the whale fishing, and the navy and the colonies, no to mention the merchant ships, men are scarce in the town. Many's the lad I've seen go and never come back.'

In spite of John's sombre statement, the two slept well during the night, Mansie free from the worry of being pressed. When they awoke in the morning, however, they heard voices below, and Mansie recognised one.

'Whist, Willie,' he said as Willie started to speak.

'Who is it?'

'The laird. He must have found out we came here.'

They lay quiet until John Stockan called them down. 'It's Mr Heddle, Mansie. He wants to speak wi' thee.'

Magnus took his contract, and descended the ladder from the attic, wary and yet wondering, and Willie followed him full of curiosity.

The laird stood near the door, and he looked a sick man. He tried to speak, and at last blurted out, 'Mansie, we're burying Harold in the morn.'

Magnus could not speak. Willie said, 'Burying Harold?'

'Yes. He ran into Peter Johnson at the cliff, to stop him catching you, and got knocked over the edge. His back was broken. We took him home, but he died shortly after. It was hours before we missed him, you see.'

Still Magnus did not speak, and the others were silent.

Alex Heddle went on in a dull voice. 'I'm paying the forty pounds. If I had only done it at once!'

Magnus spoke. 'Dunno do it. I'll go wi' the constables.'

The laird looked at Magnus. 'Harold would no like that. Come back and work for me.'

'But I've signed for the Selkirk settlement.'

'That will keep the constables off you. Come back, Magnus. I think that Harold would want you to come.'

D

The two returned to Ardvik with the laird, Magnus to resume sadly his work on the wall. In Kirkwall, Willie informed Mr Firth of what he had done. The writer asked Willie to keep on with him until mid-June and said he would give him a recommendation that would be useful should he want to be a clerk in the Hudson's Bay Company. When his time ended, Willie walked to Ardvik to spend the last few days with the minister and Mrs Peace, those kind friends with whom he always had a home.

The death of Harold he could never forget. It had come as a direct result of the white man's making of war. His father had died, and his childhood friend Ayek because of the Indians' way of war. One way seemed no better than the other. But something else within him was driving him to the Northwest, something he could not understand and regarded with misgivings. As he drew near the manse that had been his home for a time, he thought of unburdening himself to Mr Peace. But Mr Peace could not help him unless he could explain what was troubling him.

He walked past the manse until he came to a cliff from which he looked out at the long billows rolling in from the Atlantic. He wondered if the waves really rolled or did they merely rise and fall in the same place. He closed his eyes, thinking that he would know when he opened them. A picture of the prairie that rolled to the Great Northern Forest flashed into his mind, that prairie where South Branch House once stood. It appeared to be actually moving, like the waves of the sea, and he felt he was like a spar being rolled to that land as the ocean would carry a spar.

There could be no unburdening of himself to Mr Peace. He had to return to the land from which he had come.

16

A Stormy Departure

Standing on the pier at Stromness in late June, 1811, Willie Fea had a feeling like seasickness. He was, with Magnus, looking for a sign of the ship that would come and carry them across the Atlantic to Rupert's Land. Passing citizens glanced at the two young men incuriously, being used to the annual call of the Hudson's Bay vessels in June or July outward bound from London, laden with supplies, and to the call of those same ships returning in September loaded with furs for the London market. This year, only one ship, the *Prince Rupert* was to call in order to take aboard the men engaged for Lord Selkirk's proposed colony at Red River. The other two, the *Eddystone* and the *Edward and Ann* were sailing to the Hebrides to take on men at Stornoway.

It was not the sight of the sea alone that gave Willie the sick feeling, though it did remind him that over it he was returning to the land he had hoped never to see again – returning because of some inward compulsion. The death of the boy Harold hung heavily on him, though he did not see how he could have prevented it. All he had asked the boy to do was to shout 'There he is'.

If Magnus was troubled with like thoughts he said nothing. Yet Willie noted a puzzled line had deepened between the fair brows, and Magnus looked years older.

Both longed for the ship to appear; the sooner they got

away the better they would feel. Near them, a group of men, older than they, lounged by a wall in the June sun, talking loudly and guffawing when Willie or Magnus looked at them. They were also waiting for the ship, bronzed, rough-looking men who had already served in the Hudson's Bay Company or aboard whalers. Willie and Magnus had not expected companions like these; most of them were forty or over.

A coach from Kirkwall drove up, and out of it came ten young men, shy country lads who gaped at town and harbour. The loud group watched them get off, and then began to jeer.

'Haw! Haw! Green to the backbone.'

'Look at the straw in their lugs.'

The newcomers looked at the loungers and away. Seeing Willie and Magnus, a big, red-headed man lumbered over to them.

'Ken you, boys, where the agent for Lord Selkirk lives?' he asked in a drawling voice.

'Just up the street a bit,' answered Willie. 'He'll likely be here to see you, for he told me you were coming.'

'Are you for Red River?' Magnus asked.

'Aye, we're a' for Red River, but we have no contracts yet.'

'You'll soon have them,' Willie informed the man, 'for the agent wants more men badly.'

'I come from Sanday and Jock Cooper's my name. Most o' us are around Kirkwall, though.'

'I'm Mansie Isbister, and this is Willie Fea, and we're both from Ardvik.'

'Here's Captain Spence, the agent, Jock,' said Willie, as he saw the big, weather-beaten sailor approach.

'Are they for Red River?' asked Jock, nodding to the loungers.

'Aye,' muttered Magnus, 'and Lord Selkirk's got bad bargains there.'

Captain Spence had a list, and he glanced from it to the newcomers.

'Which men are you? Answer when I call your names. Murdo Rosie, Burray?'

'That's me,' said a square-built, square-headed, square-faced man.

'Say, "sir" when you answer me,' snapped the captain.

'Well, well. "Sir when you answer me", if that does any good.'

The agent's bronze face reddened, but he continued to call. 'John Cooper, Sanday?'

'That's him wi' the red hair,' wheezed Murdo, pointing.

'Each man will answer for himself, Rosie,' shouted the agent as he glared at Murdo. He continued to call until the ten were identified. Then he ordered them to come with him and he would take them to their lodgings in Stromness. They were to stand by till the ship came.

Willie and Magnus returned to the Stockan home in the evening, feeling the strain of waiting. 'I wish I were in my nook-bed in Gairstone,' murmured Magnus. 'My old mother thinks she'll never see me again.' Willie did not answer. He had visions of his mother's bones scattered where South Branch House had stood, and those of his father near by. For some years he had not allowed himself to think of that spot. They were both relieved when Mrs Stockan had supper ready. They were hungry, and eating was something to do. Both felt annoyed when a knock came to the door just as John Stockan was about to say grace, but were surprised when they heard John say, 'Aye, Willie and Mansie are here. Come in and see them.' They were still more surprised when Geordie Merriman entered.

'Geordo,' exclaimed Magnus. 'Thoo're come to see us off.'

'No, I'm comin' wi' the two o' you.'

'God's mercies! Are the constables after thee hard?'

'Aye, I never had a minute o' peace,' said Geordie.

'Sit down, Geordie, and have a bite wi' us while you speak,' invited Mrs Stockan.

'I'll be glad of it, Mrs Stockan. When Willie and you left, Magnus, it came to me that I was livin' in dread every day for a bit of poor land. Twenty acres, and here was Selkirk offerin' a hundred and more wi' nothing to pay and wi' help to get it broken out. And the constables were bound to get me in the end.'

'I did not think you would ever leave home, Geordie,' said Willie, 'but here we are, all three marked by old Nellie for better or for worse.'

'Aye,' murmured Magnus, looking at the cross on his arm. 'Mebbe it would no be right to go without Geordie.'

'What other men are comin'?' asked Geordie.

'So far as we know,' answered Magnus, 'ten young chaps from near Kirkwall, and a score or so of older men who have been to the Bay or to Greenland before. We could do without them, I'm thinkin'.'

'I took note o' them,' John Stockan said, 'and they're men that neither the Hudson's Bay nor the whalers will take on again.'

'That's no so good,' said Geordie. 'Have you heard o' this Miles Macdonell that's the head o' us?'

'He's one o' the Loyalists that would no stay in America after the revolution,' Stockan replied. 'He had been a captain in the Canadian Volunteers, and had taken land in Upper Canada after it was over. Lord Selkirk has him in London and made him governor of the new colony.'

'He'll understand the growth of the ground, then,' said Geordie.

'If we don't like it,' said Magnus, 'we can get passage back in three years and money besides.'

'Aye, and the war will be finished,' Geordie added.

'Magnus and you can come back home, but I have no home to return to.'

Willie's sad tone left the others with nothing they could think of saying until a blast of wind hit the house and wailed up between it and other houses.

'Harken to that,' said John Stockan. 'It sounds as if you boys will be here for some days yet. You'll stay wi' us too, Geordie.'

'We'll be glad to have thee,' added Mrs Stockan.

'That's ower kind o' you both,' said Geordie. 'I'll get me bag and things from the agent.'

Willie and Mansie went with Geordie into the darkness outside. The wind smote against them as they went to the harbour over which dark shadows scudded, and beyond the white crests of black waves snapped at each other, as they swirled from Scapa Flow to the Atlantic.

'Boy,' shouted Mansie above the blast, 'when it's this in the lee, any ship on the east coast will be runnin' for shelter. We'll be here for days.'

'Aye,' said Geordie, 'there'll be many a split sail in the North Sea this night.'

'We'll miss this storm at sea anyway,' Willie yelled.

It was as they feared. The Selkirk ships out from Gravesend ran to port and stayed there for two days. For four more days the three waited for the ships to appear, with time hanging drearily on them. They made friends with the young men going with them, not mixing with the old hands who hung round the ale-houses, singing and shouting insults, and harassing any one or two of the others when they were not with their crowd. Waiting did not bother them. 'The more days, the more dollars,' they said frequently.

'If Selkirk has men like them from Ireland and Scotland, ye'll have trouble waitin' for you,' said John Stockan.

'We will take it as it comes,' said Willie, recalling words of old Nellie.

In the days that followed, the two parties waiting to sail avoided one another entirely after an incident. Three young men, venturing out without their companions were provoked into a fight with three old hands who butted and kicked. Captain Spence had come on the row to settle it, and had threatened to have the offenders put in irons aboard ship if there was any repetition of fighting. In spite of his threat, the younger group still kept together lest they be attacked. When the *Prince of Wales* did arrive to take them aboard and then join the other two ships off Stornoway, the emigrants still stood in two groups, twenty-four old hands and thirty-five young men.

'Deil take it, boys,' said Geordie to the other two, 'I hoped to get clear of fightin' and we seem to have run slap into it.'

Once aboard, Geordie and the others were relieved to find that their near companions in the berths were the young men, and with lighter hearts they watched the barque crowd on sail, stand out westward, and turn south to the Hebrides to join the *Eddystone* and the *Edward and Ann*, the ships that were to embark the settlers and Company servants from Scotland and Ireland.

Their hearts were not light when they encountered the Atlantic, angry day after day. Willie, however, had a sad feeling of companionship with the vessel. Across the angry ocean it was driven by forces it could not resist.

17

A Forbidding Land

Late on a cold September day in 1811 over a hundred men stood huddled in groups, chilled by an icy wind, on the low shore of Hudson's Bay. Outside at the river mouth lay the three ships that had taken them across the Atlantic. For sixty-one days these ships had been battered by wind and storm in one of the longest voyages on record. In them the men now on the shore had been crammed together suffering from seasickness, bad food, disease, and general ill-will. They had longed for the land which had been held out to them as a land of promise. Landward lay a cheerless view of sand and rock, and sparse and scrubby vegetation, and seaward a dirty expanse of sand and a dull sea.

'Well,' drawled Jock Cooper, 'we have our feet on land again.'

'Aye,' said Magnus, pale yet from his sickness on the voyage, 'such as it is, I'm glad to be on it.'

'If this is what the ground's like, I will be glad to get back to Orkney,' Geordie added.

'Bless thee, Geordie, we have a thousand miles to go to get to Captain Macdonell's Promised Land,' wheezed Murdo Rosie, 'but if it's as hard to get to as it was gettin' here, I'll be back wi' thee.'

Willie heard his friends speak while his eyes swept from the rocks and scrub to the dull sea. His memory held no recollection of this view, but only a faint recalling of the terror that had numbed him here as a child. He viewed it with misgivings, but he had no wish now to be back in Orkney. Whatever lay beyond the southern skyline, the rivers and the broad prairie called him, and there, in spite of his forebodings, he must go and never return. His Orkney roots had been pulled out.

Miles Macdonell stood on a low rock and barked out commands to get into lines. His dark countenance and harsh features were grimmer than usual. No one had come to meet him from the near-by fort, standing on high ground within its palisade. He ordered his men forward, and led them to the gate. They followed in twos and threes, over the track, with the slow, deliberate steps of the labourer. Outside the gate Macdonell shouted an order to halt, and the hundred odd men stopped walking. Macdonell and his four officers went into York Factory – as the fort was called – leaving the men shuffling about outside.

They gathered in groups; the rather superior clerks from Glasgow, the Irish, the few Scottish Gaelic-speakers, and the Orkneymen still keeping to their two groups. A few men from Inverness and Ross joined the young Orkney group.

'This is goin' to be worse than the ship,' observed Jock Cooper.

'Gid-gad forbid,' murmured Magnus. He recalled his mother's parting words. 'Mansie, I'll never see thee again.' Did she feel he would die before her?

Hungry and cold, they had nothing more to say. After a long wait, Macdonell came with a Company officer, both grim.

'The craw isa' a colour wi' the corbie,' wheezed Murdo, his grey eyes beneath pulled-down eyebrows eyeing the two.

'Men,' shouted Macdonell, 'you'll be given tents and

someone will show you how to pitch them. I'll see about food for you as soon as possible.'

'Sir,' said one of the old hands, 'we signed for the Company, and we are entitled by our contracts to Company quarters and food.'

'You were signed for the Company or for the Settlement,' snapped Macdonell, 'and will be duly assigned to one or the other.'

'But the agent in Stromness . . .'

'What the devil was your agent in Stromness doing in signing that man, Captain Macdonell?' growled the Company officer. 'He was sent home ineffective some years ago, and is fifty if he's a day.'

Macdonell scowled. 'Your agent in Stromness signed him, Mr Auld, not me. Men, get yourselves in groups of ten, and be ready for the tents.'

The old hands made sure they got the first tents. The very last group to get one was Willie and his friends. A wrinkled, yellow-skinned old man went with them for it, and showed them where it was to be pitched. Silently he set up the poles, tepee-fashion, signing when he wanted help, and when they were up, indicating to the men that these poles must be firm. Again a memory came to Willie. He had seen this done before. The old man signed for help to shake out some hides, and had them wrapped around and fastened to the poles. When this was finished, he went silently away.

Willie's group waited. Nothing was said for no one had a cheery word left or any desire to talk. At last they were taken inside the palisade and given a rough meal of salt pork, no better than what they had had aboard ship. Then they stood outside their home of hide, looking glumly from swamps and rocks to the leaden sea and the ships at anchor five miles out. After a few hours ashore, most felt they would like to be aboard these miserable ships on a homeward voyage. Night fell, and they huddled into their tents, sleeping in their rough clothes, feet towards the centre, and warmed by the proximity of their companions. Willie was the last to lie down. The stoicism of his mother's people now possessed him. Hunger and cold he had known as a child; he heeded them now as little as he had done the blows of the gyro.

Next day during a lull in the carrying of the cargo from the boats to the fort, Magnus and Geordie were standing by themselves, straightening their backs, when a large man approached with slow, ponderous steps looking over the men. He was evidently an officer of the Company, though his deerskin trousers and moccasins, his blue capote, and his grizzled hair was little like the imposing dress of Mr Auld. Magnus was sure he had seen him before, the large nose and craggy features, the bushy eyebrows, and the big body, now stooped. 'Who's that man?' he whispered to Geordie. Geordie stared, saw the red waist-coat beneath the capote, and exclaimed, 'It's Mr Tomison.' The big man heard and looked hard at the two. Magnus was noting how the man had aged.

'Where do you come from?' he asked gruffly.

'From Orkney, sir,' answered Magnus.

'You have seen me before?'

'At Nether Ardvik, Mr Tomison,' Geordie hastened to say, 'in the harvest when you came to see Willie.'

'Willie Fea! What's the boy doing now?'

'He's there, sir,' said Magnus, seeing Willie lay down a burden. 'I'll get him.'

Magnus hurried over. 'Willie, Mr Tomison wants to speak to thee ower there.'

Willie straightened the bundles, and went with Magnus. He felt shy again of meeting Tomison. It was not his former aloofness, but here was his father's friend who had paid for his education finding him a labourer. As he walked, he felt remorse. The aged man in front of him was shrunk from his former rock-like form, and the grey hairs that straggled down from his tam-o'-shanter showed him to be old and worn. When Tomison held out a large hand, Willie grasped it.

'Willie, boy, have they not made you a clerk?' asked Tomison.

'Not yet, sir, though there's a kind of promise from Captain Spence.'

'I doubt if his promise will matter here, Willie, and my word would go against you now. You can write, I think.'

'Yes, I served with Mr Firth in Kirkwall for a time.'

'You'll be a clerk soon, then.'

'Just now, I'd sooner go with my two friends here as a labourer. I have not seen much I like in the officers.'

'No, you wouldn't. They've pushed me aside here since I came back, me that was once their master. But I'm against the rum trade, and the Company think it's the only way to compete with the Northwesters. They're ruining the Indians, and also my life work here for the Company.' I'm going home, Willie, for I'm a done man, and seventy-two years of age. I'll speak to Miles Macdonell about you. And the three of you, stand by Macdonell, for he's the only honest man you'll meet here. The Hudson's Bay men don't want the settlement; it will fail, they think, and they'll get you into their service just as they need you. The other company, the Nor'westers, stick at nothing. They've been frightening the Indians and the Hudson's Bay men for years, for they have ten men for every one the Hudson's

Bay have. You'll get trouble from the Northwesters or I'm mistaken. I see they're calling you to work. Good-bye, boys, and the good Lord be with you.'

He shook hands with all three, and limped away. Willie watched him sadly, thinking that the old man would even be deprived of leaving his bones in the Northwest.

'Come on, you bloody Orkneymen,' shouted an officer. 'We have no favourites here.'

Next day, they prepared to go up the Nelson to build winter quarters, for the rivers would soon be frozen, and they could not reach Red River till next year. On the straggling march of twenty miles up the left bank, the men, sweating under heavy loads, joked between curses.

'Wi' Moses, forty years in the wilderness,' wheezed Murdo, and all but Willie laughed. He remembered the other wilderness that held bitter memories.

18

The Promised Land

Almost a year later, two large sailing-boats and a clumsy barge-type vessel were being rowed over the placid waters of Red River. It was late August of 1812.

On the bateau, as Governor Macdonell called the barge, Murdo Rosie, Magnus Isbister, William Fea, and George Merriman handled oars and square sail while keeping an eye on the bull and cow which had been purchased at Oxford House on the way from Hudson's Bay. These cattle had been their care over half the seven hundred miles and over many of the rapids and falls which they had traversed in the journey upstream.

Willie Fea was thinking of the troubles that had beset the venture since it started; the miserable Atlantic crossing, the cold and hungry winter, the bickerings of the officers of the settlement with those of the Hudson's Bay Company, fights between different groups of men, and the rebellion against authority. He and his friends had kept out of the violence, but they were left with little liking for the venture. Of the hundred odd men who had come out, less than thirty were in the boats. Seventy had gone to the Hudson's Bay service, some had been sent home to be tried for assault and rebellion, and one had died of scurvy. Willie's friends, however, seemed to think their troubles were ended.

'Weel,' said Murdo in his quick, rasping way, 'Captain Macdonell's promised land looks not so bad after all.'

'It can only be better than we've seen,' answered Magnus, 'and we can't be worse off than we've been.'

'Aye, we starved and froze all the winter,' agreed Geordie, 'and the Irish and that coarse lot from Stromness did nothing but fight. But the trees are bonny here, and the land seems grand since we left the swamps.'

Willie Fea's eyes swept from bank to bank, and occasionally he caught glimpses of the flat plain stretching westward. These glimpses alone reminded him of the land which he remembered; little in the journey had been familiar, for he remembered nothing of his journey to York Factory from Cumberland House in 1795. But even the plain was utterly flat, not rolling prairie as it was where South Branch House had stood. In spite of his friends' comments, a dull ache lay at his heart.

A point of land hid the view up Red River, and on the side they could see a number of Indians standing and staring. The boats drew in, and the oarsmen rested on oars. Willie listened along with the others to the halting Cree of Macdonell, a language he had picked up again at York Factory.

'We come in peace,' said Macdonell to the leader.

'Peace from Peguis, Chief of the Saulteaux,' the leader answered.

'We build a fort near,' went on Macdonell.

'We come and bring meat and fish,' answered Peguis.

'We thank you, and may you kill many buffalo.'

The chief shook his head. 'Bad men run the buffalo away.'

'Sioux Indian?' asked Macdonell.

'No. Not Indian, not paleface. Hunter of fur men.'

'Oh, the half-breeds. Come to see us, Peguis.'

'Peguis come soon.'

The boats moved on, and rounded the point. On their right stood a set of buildings inside a stockade. The boats drew in to the left where some tents were pitched, and the bateau pushed into the shallow water. Captain Macdonell, standing on the bank, ordered his men to unload.

The cow, led by Magnus and followed by Willie, heaved her forelegs over the side of the bateau and lifted her hind legs over. Eve, as the animal was called, was in Macdonell's garden of Eden before her mate. Geordie held Adam, the bull, straining after the cow. He took the side with a bound, but his hind leg got caught on it. 'Hold, ye Jezebel,' rasped Murdo as he seized the kicking foot and, on the upward swing, heaved it clear. Adam, now with Eve, turned his head to look placidly at the men.

'He's no a bad beast, Murdo, and can't be what you called him,' said Jock Cooper, who had come with others from the boats to help in unloading the bateau.

'Well, Jock, we've planted Adam and Eve here. Where's the serpent?'

'Give him time, Murdo. Like thee, he's in no hurry.'

Geordie had taken a hoe, and began to tear up the soil while the others watched the black earth appear. 'No sign o' clay, boys. It's as black as the devil's waistcoat.'

'Give him time, Geordie,' said Murdo dryly. 'He'll be here for his waistcoat.

'Somebody's planted tatties there,' remarked Magnus, pointing to a patch of weeds and potato tops, 'but never hoed them.'

While they talked, Willie was looking westward over the plain. He knew it stretched beyond the horizon, mile

E

after mile, to the mountains from which the Saskatchewan flowed. A spot there was pulling him more and more. Some day he would wander beyond the horizon, but it must be alone.

The men busied themselves with the unloading. 'Did you see any teeth for the harrow, Murdo?' asked Geordie.

'Harrow, Geordie. Captain Macdonell has handles for the hoes. Why bother wi' a harrow.'

'The hooks he has might catch a minnow but no the fish in the river,' grumbled Magnus.

'He's aye telling us to learn to use our hands,' rasped Murdo. 'I see no sign o' net or twine.'

When the boats were unloaded, the men began to wander around. 'Pitch your tents, men,' shouted Macdonell, and the men, now used to the job, pitched their six tents alongside those of the Hudson's Bay men who were waiting for the carts to take them westward to their posts. The fort over the river, at the junction of the Assiniboine, was that of the rival Northwest Company, and the men in it were watching closely the doings of the settlers. With their tents pitched, the settlers stood in groups conversing, the Irish and a few Highlanders in Gaelic, the men from the south of Scotland and from Orkney in their various dialects.

They were surprised when a noise sounded from the south. A group of horsemen, scattering dust and shouting war whoops galloped furiously towards them. Surprise gave place to alarm.

'The devil's comin' for his waistcoat, Geordie,' muttered Murdo.

As the wild-looking horsemen drew near, they fired guns in the air and brandished spears and tomahawks, yelling savagely.

THE PROMISED LAND 115

'Mighty! Lord! This is the finish of us,' mumbled Geordie.

Willie's first feeling was one of panic, but he forced it back. He looked closely at the horsemen. 'These are not Indians,' he shouted.

'They're going to kill us anyway,' Magnus muttered.

The little party huddled together, expecting to be cut down, when the horsemen jerked to a stop some twenty paces away. Miles Macdonell strode in front of his men. 'What do you want?' he demanded harshly.

'You come to take our father's land,' cried a spokesman. 'Go or we kill you. This land is ours.'

'Go yourselves,' cried Macdonell. 'This land is not yours. You are not Indians but creatures of the Northwest Company decked out to frighten us. You're not frightening me.'

'This land is not yours. You go or we shoot.'

Macdonell's officers had been hurriedly handing out small arms to the men, and directing brass swivel guns at the horsemen.

'See these cannon,' thundered Macdonell. 'Begone or they speak.'

The spokesman of the horsemen turned to his men, and a mumbling followed, while six cannon were directed to the mock Indians. The muttering stopped, and the horsemen turned away shouting 'Chiens'. They galloped away to the south.

'The serpent has slithered away, Murdo,' said Jock Cooper. 'Say as you like, Macdonell's no easy frightened.'

'But I was,' said Geordie in relief. 'I thought my last minute had come.'

'Men,' shouted Macdonell, 'that was a bluff of the Northwest half-breeds to frighten us. Expect such tricks from time to time. They enjoy frightening people when they can. Stand firm and never show fear. We are here by right. If they dare attack us, we shall show them the stuff we are made of.'

'Aye,' muttered Murdo, 'and wi' our hands, for this gun was stuck in my hand and nothing to load into it.'

'It would do for a club, Murdo,' said Jock. 'I had my empty hands and my feet in two holey boots.'

'Were thoo no frightened, Mansie?' enquired Geordie.

'I was sure we were to be killed. Why did they no look Indian, Willie?' asked Magnus.

'Indians don't come like that,' answered Willie, 'with bridles on their horses and not rope halters. They fired in the air, too.'

'All I saw was wild-like men,' declared Geordie, now over his fear.

'Come for your food, men,' shouted an officer, and each man got a hard biscuit and a piece of greasy pemmican. After eating this, the men quenched their thirst at the river. Then they were set to work, some to fish and some to turn over the soil with hoes.

'Willie Fea!' yelled Macdonell, and Willie approached the dark, stern governor, wondering why he had been called.

'I heard you tell the men those were not Indians, Fea. I hear you were born in the country, and escaped from South Branch House.'

'That is so, sir.'

'Mr Tomison told me at York Factory that you were well educated and had served as a writer.'

'Yes, sir.'

'Check these supplies and each bit of equipment every man gets. I already have too many officers for the number of men, but I'll make you a clerk as soon as I can. I may also need you as interpreter. You have worked well so far, but you must remain a labourer for a time. You know how unfortunate we've been.'

'Yes, sir, I have tasted it all,' murmured Willie.

'I go to pay our respects to the gentlemen in Fort Gibraltar, over there. See to it that the men are diligent in their duties.'

Macdonell turned away without waiting for an answer. Willie, checking the supplies on the sheets given him, found more missing than on the bank. There were axe heads without handles, no twine for making nets, no nets, only a few hoes, and one spade. He felt low in himself; what was needed here had been lost or stolen en route. He decided not to tell his friends how bad the situation was. Macdonell certainly needed a competent clerk. He walked around to where men were turning up the sun-baked earth with hoes. They straightened their backs as he approached, and Willie was prepared to get jocular or sarcastic remarks. But he got none. One asked him to tell the Governor that hoes could not prepare the soil well for a growing crop. When he came to Jock and Murdo, he was complimented on his new job, and he hastened to tell them it was only for the evening.

'If this harrow had teeth, we could yoke the bull and cow to it,' said Jock.

'What, Jock?' demanded Murdo. 'Use a beast for what a man can do! Learn to use your hands, men. I've fished all my life and I'm put to the hoe.'

'I might get a chance to mention to the Governor that fishermen are good at catching fish,' laughed Willie.

'Aye and he'll ask if they can do it with their hands.'

Willie passed on to where Magnus and Geordie were

fishing. Magnus had caught three fair-sized white fish, but Geordie hadn't caught any. 'They put me to fishing that never fished,' complained Geordie, 'and they put Murdo to the hoe that never farmed.'

'What's wrong, Geordie, is the hook,' Magnus explained. 'These hooks are for small fish.'

'There's no large hooks,' said Willie. 'When the Governor knows, he may get some from the Hudson's Bay men.'

The officers returned, and the men turned in for the night. Next day, Willie was questioned by an officer about his check, and had to go over it again with him, but it was found accurate. Then Willie went to the hoe with Jock and Murdo. He felt more at ease with them, and wondered if he were made a clerk it would mean losing his friends. He had lost all his relations. For a few days the men lived on the handful of fish caught, and on the potatoes planted earlier on the orders of the Hudson's Bay company. On 4 September, they were given a holiday.

The men had erected a flag-pole, and were drawn up near it. By the pole stood Miles Macdonell and his four officers in cloaks, and near them three officers of the Northwest Company, invited over to watch the ceremony. Farther off stood a group of Saulteaux Indians with their chief, Peguis. Apart from them were a number of half-breed servants of the Northwest Company employed at Fort Gibraltar, and near them some half-breeds not employed by either company who lived by hunting and trapping. These stayed near the forts in winter, and were known as freemen since they were free to take service with either company. Governor Macdonell, standing under the flag, read a mandate which granted the land to Lord Selkirk. Having rolled up the parchment, he ordered the cannon to be fired as he took possession as Lord Selkirk's agent. Then he called for three cheers, the officers answering heartily, the men raggedly, not being used to the game. Then he and his officers along with those of the Northwest Company went to his tent to partake of gentlemen's refreshment – the wines had not been left behind. The Indians and half-breeds, not speaking English, went away wondering if these white newcomers worshipped a pole.

'Well, well,' rasped Murdo. 'Lord Selkirk's money wasted on feeding gutsy Orkneymen, as he once complained.'

'Ah but a dram's comin' for us, Murdo,' said Jock Cooper, pointing to an officer carrying a small keg of rum. The keg being broached, each man was given a stiff drink. Willie, however, gave his to his friends, and spoke little and laughed none in that day of jollity. He stood by the river looking westward and northward. Up there lay the bones of his parents. His grandparents' bones lay in the kirkyard at Ardvik, safe and secure. His ties to the island were all snapped. All except the memory of Harold.

Next morning, Peguis and some of his Saulteaux came, bringing gifts of fish and meat. Willie noted them closely. They seemed peaceful and friendly, not the least like the frenzied Gros Ventres whom he had pictured all along as the Indians. His mother's people, the Cree, were close kinsmen of the Saulteaux.

Two days later, the party left and set off up the Red River to Pembina Forks, where there would be plenty of buffalo for the winter. They had found no supplies left by the Hudson's Bay Company as had been hoped, only the potato patch. Macdonell had expected a store of pemmican. On the journey up the river, Willie gave all his attention to the oar, and spoke only in answer to Magnus who rowed with him.

'Willie, boy,' asked Magnus gently, 'what's bothering you?'

Willie did not answer.

'They should have made you a clerk.'

'It's not that, Magnus. The boy, Harold. I can't forget.'

'Gid-gad, Willie. You did not push him ower the crag.'

'No, but my trick caused his death.'

'Aye. It was for me. It bothers me, too, but we're no to blame. It was providence, Willie, and put it out o' your mind.'

'You're likely right, Mansie, and I'll try.'

19

Struggle to Live

About six weeks after the newcomers had arrived at Pembina Forks, Willie was again called on to do a clerk's work, or at least to go round with Macdonell to take notes. They walked rapidly round the new storehouse and half a dozen shacks to house the men, and then to where axemen were setting up new buildings. Still to be built were a residence for the Governor and his officers and more shacks for a large number of settlers who were expected soon. Macdonell had named the buildings Fort Daer, to honour Lord Selkirk whose family name it was. At one of the shacks, Macdonell stopped to watch Jock Cooper who had been put to the job of notching because skilled axemen were scarce. He noted that Cooper, who had won his favour by his strength in lifting boats over shoals, was using an adze with a three-foot handle.

'Cooper, why are you not using an axe?' he asked.

'I can use this better, sir.'

'In this country, Cooper, the axe is the tool. Take it up.'

'Sir,' said an axeman, 'he notches with that as quick as we do with the axe. We had to wait for him when he used the axe.'

'Oh, very well then. You are not a carpenter, Cooper. Where did you learn to use that?'

'Helpin' a ship's carpenter pile a pier, one time.'

'I see, but learn to use the axe, Cooper.'

As he passed on, Jock grinned to Willie, who followed Macdonell to the woods. Murdo Rosie was trying to cut down a tree.

'Where will that tree fall, my man?' asked the Governor, looking all around.

Murdo winked at Willie. 'Deed, Captain, the Lord gave me no gift o' prophecy,' he answered.

'But he gave you a head,' snapped Macdonell. 'Give me your axe. You see that clear space. Slash the tree on the side opposite, like this. Then notch it on the side next the space, like this,' said the Governor, making the chips fly. 'And swing your axe. Don't hack. Do you see?' And he handed Murdo the axe.

'Aye, Captain, and someone might have shown me this a year ago.'

'You could have watched the axemen,' snapped Macdonell, and passed on to where Geordie Merriman, Magnus Isbister, and two others were carrying out a large log. He watched Magnus stagger under the weight at the front end. When they put down the log, he said, 'Isbister, who put you to this? You are too small for this work. Change with Rosie.'

'But I can't use the axe, sir.'

'Learn, man. You must.'

'It's not that, sir, but I cut my foot and . . . Hark!'

All the men near straightened up and listened. At first they could hear nothing.

'What did you hear, Isbister?'

'There, sir, the bagpipes.'

All could hear it now, a slow march, sad and plaintive. Across the river horsemen approached, and behind the piper a long string of people. The horsemen were French half-breeds and Indians, who were guiding the new settlers to Pembina Forks. They wound slowly nearer; men, some women with children on their backs, some with loads, a few boys and girls, about seventy people in all. They were walking slowly, heavily burdened, and they dragged their feet in the short prairie grass.

'Stop work, men,' commanded Miles Macdonell. 'Help these people across the river.'

The horses were already splashing through the shallow water. The piper marched slowly in, piping as he splashed. Willie, followed by the other men hurried down the steep bank and waded through the water to the newcomers. Geordie approached a woman with a baby on her back, and reached out to take the child. The woman turned on him furiously.

'Away, ye heathen,' she screamed. 'Ye'll not take me child again, ye villain.'

'Heathen!' exclaimed Geordie. 'Wumman, I'm no heathen, but Geordie Merriman that Captain Macdonell sent to help ye.'

'Glory be, and is yon the place, and are we rid of the heathen guides that ran off with me baby once?'

'Aye, and welcome here, poor as it is. You'll be ower tired.'

'Bless your honest face. Go to the man, Biddy.' And she handed over the child, who, on the journey, had been carried away by a horseman as a joke, and returned.

Willie had gone straight to a ten-year-old boy staggering under the burden of a two-year-old girl.

'I'll carry your sister, lad. You seem very tired.'

The boy, ragged and footsore, his feet dragging through the water, looked up at Willie, and held his sister out. Moisture came into Willie's dried-up eyes as the little girl put her arms round his neck and leaned her brown hair against his cheek. He felt the boy's warm hand in his free one, and stepped carefully out of the water and up the bank. Magnus was following with a bundle which he had taken from the shoulders of the pale and worn-looking mother. They came to the storehouse and surrounding huts, and put down their burdens.

The rest of the day was declared a holiday. All were given a special meal of buffalo meat, and after the meal, rum was served. The new arrivals were visited by the old, learning names and home parishes. The cares of the emigrants, new and old, seemed to drop from them, and in the gloaming of an October day, the piper played reels and the people danced. Willie forgot for a time his sorrow, and danced a reel, his opposite being the boy he had helped from the river, Malcolm McPherson.

For the remainder of the year, the women tried to make the interiors of the shacks comfortable with the few blankets and the many buffalo hides they had, and when they could, they made little stools and pole beds. The hunters had no trouble in finding meat, for the brown herds of buffalo browsed on the prairie grass close to Fort Daer. The men kept busy building the Governor's residence, and more shacks, plastering the chinks with poles and wet clay, and cutting firewood. By Christmas, when the cold grew extreme, all were housed. After New Year, snow lay deep on the plains.

The buffalo herds moved farther away from the fort, and the hunters had to go farther and farther to find them. Consequently they were slower in bringing in the meat. When they did return with a kill Macdonell ordered them to put the meat up on raised pole platforms, safe from wild animals. The herds were now feeding and sheltering in the thickets and at the edges of woods, and from there the settlers had to fetch the meat on foot. Many of them, unaware of the intensity of the cold, suffered frozen hands and feet in bringing it in. Otherwise, they fared well until the New Year was seven weeks old. Magnus stopped worrying about Willie, who seemed to have shed his depression with the arrival of the settlers from the Hebrides and Sligo, and was pleased to be given the job of going with a hunter to learn how to hunt.

A bad blizzard in late February, however, brought privation to all. Some of the experienced hunters lost their lives far out on the plain where winds whipped up the snow as it fell, reducing visibility to twenty yards even when eyes and nostrils were not clogged. Willie had returned from hunting before the blizzard started, and was ready to go off again when it blew itself out. The plight of the women and children, however, and the shortage of food convinced Macdonell that some of the men and their families should be moved nearer the haunts of the buffalo, and he sent Willie, with Magnus and Geordie, to guide the McNeills and the MacPhersons, the two families whom they had helped across the Pembina, up the river to an old fort. The two husbands were suffering from frost-bite, their feet aching.

They set off early in March on a cold, pale morning with a slight wind blowing bitingly from the north. The men were loaded with blankets, hides, a kettle, two axes, some candles, flint and steel, and Willie had an old musket, with some powder and shot. He led the way, heavily loaded, and the boy Malcolm followed him. Behind came Magnus, also loaded, the two women with their babies, and the two men with lighter loads because of painful feet. Geordie, with the heaviest load, was the last man. Weakened from the want of food, suffering from the cold, and with despair in the hearts of the parents, they plodded in Willie's tracks, hour after hour, mile after painful mile, frequently having to stop until the cold drove them on again. Often Willie looked behind at the mothers, but he could only help if he discarded part of his load, and all of it was needed if they were to live. Their shadows, thrown by a cold sun up in a pitiless blue sky gradually slanted from straight northeastward on the unmarked snow that stretched to their right; only the line of trees and shrubs that marked the Pembina on their left broke that white expanse. Slowly their shadows fell behind, while the mothers and the men feared for the lives of the little girl and the baby, who whimpered from time to time, being cold, hungry, and weak.

The sun began to sink in the west, its pale yellow shining bright in their eyes. Then it went out of sight, and a bluish tint spread over the immense whiteness.

'Oh, Davie, I canna go on,' moaned Mrs McPherson, sinking with her child into the snow.

Her husband looked at her in despair. 'But lass, ye must. The bairns, ye ken.'

Mrs McPherson breathed heavily. She murmured, 'Help me up. I'll take a step, and another, and another.'

Geordie, Magnus, and Willie had gathered round. 'Stay with them, boys,' said Willie, and keep them moving slowly. Magnus, set the pace. 'I'll go ahead, for I think we're near.'

'Aye, and light a fire, Willie,' said Magnus.

'Malcolm, can you carry my musket and these horns of shot?'

'Aye, and I'll come with ye,' said the boy.

Willie moved on, followed by the boy, to hear Geordie's

voice saying, 'Keep your hearts up, laddies. Willie says it's no far now.'

Willie and the boy went on in the gathering darkness, the air getting slightly warmer. They came to an old palisade, and into an enclosure of five old cabins. Willie put down his load and told Malcolm to search the cabins for buffalo meat. Inside one with a stone and clay chimney he lit a fire, and Malcolm came to say there was meat in one cabin. Willie went to get some, and by the time he got it, the party were at the door. Hastily the three friends shook out some buffalo hides, and the wearied wives and husbands sank down with the two babies.

Willie filled the large kettle with snow and into the melting waters put the frozen meat. It was long before it boiled, and the eyes of women and children were closing and opening slowly. At last they were able to eat the warm meat, the baby getting the brew. All huddled together in the one cabin for that night, and slept fitfully, waking from time to time, feeling they were dragging their legs through the snow.

20

Noo, thee, Peerie Mansie

During March, 1813, the three friends with the McPhersons and the McNeills lived harmoniously and monotonously in the old fort. They did not themselves hunt buffalo, for the old musket given to Willie was to be used only for emergencies. Macdonell had hired more freemen – men not engaged by fur companies – experienced in hunting, and they left the animals they killed on raised stages for the settlers to find. McPherson and McNeill, both still troubled with their frozen feet, kept near the river where they would not get lost, and Willie, Magnus, and Geordie searched for the meat stores on the plain to the north and the north-west. The snow had gone by mid-March except for crystal scatterings at the roots of the prairie grass, and the little company hoped that the long winter was over, the rivers would flow, the geese return, and they would have fish and fowl to vary the buffalo meat.

Late in the month a blizzard blew up suddenly and lasted for three days. The meat supply had been low before it started, and the two wives had rationed the party to one meal a day. When the storm blew itself out, no meat was left, and the men set off to search. Nothing was found on the first day. The snow lay deep, travelling was difficult, and any hunters who had been out before the blizzard could not have survived. Once again starvation faced the party in the old fort.

'Magnus,' said Willie, 'I'm off to Fort Daer in the morning. I'll leave the musket with you. Keep on looking, though I have no hope of your finding anything.'

'But will they have anything there, Willie?'

'They'll have to by the time I get there, or they'll be starving themselves.'

'That's true, and we'll keep at it here, only I wish Davie and Andrew would stay wi' their wives. Their feet's no that good.'

'Let them search, Magnus, or they'll feel bad about it. You will easily find them if anything happens.'

Willie was away before dawn. The others found that it had warmed up a little, and the men prepared to leave, the boy Malcolm with them. They left the women, with the two babies, and trailed out by the river. The snow was hardened in drifts and hollows varying in depths from three feet to two inches, as if the white breakers of the sea had been suddenly frozen. When Mansie and Geordie left the men to go north, the boy wanted to go with them, and followed them for some time before the men noticed. Malcolm looked sullen when Magnus ordered him back, but turned in his tracks and dragged his feet back towards the river. Waiting long enough to see that the boy kept going back, the two friends again set out north and west. Hour after hour they searched, cutting across the waves of snow, on and on. They rested from time to time, their feet cold and painful, while a cold sun shone on them and the vast white surface, without much warmth in it. Then they plodded on until the sun began to sink in the west.

'I'm nigh done, Mansie,' groaned Geordie during one rest.

'So am I, but I don't want to face the bairns again wi' nothing.'

'The hunters would no be out yet. I fear there's nothing to find.'

'Maybe no. Start back, Geordie, or stay here if thoo're clean done. I'll go on a bit.'

'Ill try a bit again, but my legs are weak.'

On they dragged their way over and between the drifts. The sky began to cloud over, and at first they thought darkness was coming, but they caught a glimpse of the yellow sun through the drifting cloud wrack. The air grew warmer, and they rested for a time, feeling hopeless, and thinking of the pale and pinched faces back at the old fort.

At last they spied a snow-covered hump, and hastened to it. Hurriedly they cleared away the snow to uncover a buffalo skin within which was buffalo meat. Some entrails were scattered untouched in the hollows, showing that no wolves had been there. Eagerly they took what they could carry, covered the remainder with the hide, and kicked snow over it. Burdened with the meat, they began to follow their tracks back while dark shadows crept over the snow from the east.

They had to rest often, their legs weary, their feet painful. In silence they dragged on, their paces growing short. Darkness now covered the snow. The Pleides shone on their left, Orion rose in front, and the Plough showed dimly behind. Now they had to leave their tracks, since they could no longer pace as they had done, and keeping the North Star over their left shoulders, they dragged their way through the unmarked snow. At last, a faint brick-red light appeared for a moment, and disappeared. The dim outline of the fort appeared. Someone had opened a door and closed it, giving them one gleam of candlelight.

'Boy, Mansie,' said Geordie, breaking the silence, 'they'll be blithe to see us.'

Magnus did not speak. He went to the McPherson door and pushed it open, crying, 'We found meat.'

He got no answer, and looked at Mrs McPherson who held her little girl. The woman's face wore a look of agony. He looked at Davie McPherson who was staring at the ground, and muttered, 'You saw no sign of Malcolm.'

'Malcolm!' exclaimed Geordie. 'Mansie sent him back to you, and we saw him go.'

'Aye, he came to us and followed behind, and we forgot him. When we turned around, he was no there.'

'My poor laddie. He'll be torn to bits by the wild beasts,' wailed Mrs McPherson.

Magnus felt his limbs shake under him as he looked at the father and mother. He said, 'Don't think that yet, Mrs McPherson. Malcolm has good sense, and the night's no cold. We can't seek him in the dark, and Geordie and me can go no more this day. We'll try in the morn.'

'Were you far out when you missed him?' asked Geordie.

'Far,' said Davie, 'and Andrew and I hunted and hunted, but could find no trace o' him. We came back, hoping he had gone to you.'

'We never saw a sign o' him,' said Geordie. 'He must be near the river.'

'We hunted there. I doubt my first-born is gone.'

'There were no wild beasts around that we saw,' said Magnus. 'Don't give up heart. We'll look in the mornin'.'

The family seemed a little comforted, and the McNeills had the meat on cooking. But it was a sad group that huddled round the wood fire below the clumsy chimney. When Geordie and Magnus went to their shack, they sat in silence for a time, then Geordie lay down, saying, 'We'll be off early, Mansie.' Magnus did not answer, he sat upright and still.

When Geordie awoke next morning, there was no Magnus beside him. He went out. Much of the snow had melted, and a skim of ice covered some newly-formed pools. He went to the shack containing the families. Magnus was not there, and they had not seen him. 'Mighty,' exclaimed Geordie, 'he's away on an empty belly, and him clean done last night. We'll eat afore we go, or we'll no get far.'

Soon the three men were on their way, each leg-weary and foot-sore. No tracks were to be seen. After travelling for hours, the sun now in the south, they rested, and saw someone coming towards them. They hurried on, Geordie muttering, 'Mansie would no come back wantin' the boy.' As the figure neared, they saw it was Malcolm. They could hear now the scraping of his horn moccasins, and saw he was far spent.

'Malcolm laddie, where have ye been?' called Davie to his son.

The boy dragged his way to his father and stood silent for a minute. Then he whispered throatily, his eyes on the ground, 'When I left you, I went after Geordie and Magnus again and lost my way. I turned back to the river, and it grew dark. I lay under a pine tree all night, too frightened to go to sleep, Father.'

'Laddie, laddie,' said his father, 'your mother and me have had a sore night. It was sinful of ye.'

Malcolm began to cry. Geordie asked, 'Did you see Mansie, Malcolm?'

'No,' sobbed the boy, 'I wondered why he was not with you.'

The group stood silent for a minute. Then Geordie said, 'He'll have passed Malcolm mebbe in the dark. Take Malcolm back to his mother, and I'll find Mansie.'

'Sure and I'll come with ye, Geordie,' said Andrew McNeill. 'Davie must go and set his wife's mind at rest.'

So two went on and two went back. After a while, Andrew said, 'The young devil must have left us hereabouts.' They scanned the ground for a while and McNeill found in the little remaining snow two sets of tracks leading north. 'Here's where the boy went, and Mansie must have followed this way. The boy must have come back to the river near where we met him this morning.'

'We'll go north as the tracks point,' said Geordie, 'and should see him soon. A body sees a long way on this plain.'

They went on, looking far to the north, and far to the west, but only the plain and the sky met their eyes. Not a sign of a track. Legs tired and feet sore, they kept on until the sun began to sink. Then they turned back, and dragged their way to the fort, arriving in the dark. The group round the wood fire were cheerless again that night. All next day Davie McPherson and Geordie searched, McNeill being too far spent to go. Again they returned in the dark with no Magnus.

'It's no use, folks,' Geordie mumbled. 'If Mansie were livin', he'd be back here. He could no' last and him near starvin' when he set out.'

Geordie went to his cold shack. No Magnus and no Willie. But Willie would come, and learn about Magnus whom he loved as a brother.

'But his poor old folk when they ken.' moaned Geordie.

21

Bones on the Prairie

Towards the end of the fourth day after he had left, Willie Fea was returning to the old fort. Burdened with fifty pounds of buffalo meat, he was very tired, but he cheered himself with the thought of what his arrival would bring to the two families and his two friends. He had gone with the buffalo hunters until they made a kill, and had returned as straight as he could to the fort, leaving the rest of the meat cached for other settlers to fetch to their families at Fort Daer. In the evening, he came in sight of the old fort and quickened his pace. He saw no one around. Coming to the door of the cabin with the chimney that contained the families, he pushed open the door. 'Meat, Andrew and Davie.'

No one answered at first. The two men and the two women gazed sadly at him. Malcolm looked through tear-stained eyes. As Willie was about to ask what was wrong, Davie McPherson said, 'Aye, we have some already and are likely to choke on it.'

'Why? What's wrong?' asked Willie anxiously.

Geordie had come from his shack and stood by him. 'Willie boy, he's gone.'

Willie dropped his load. 'Magnus? Is he dead?'

'He wandered off lookin' for Malcolm before the rest of us got up, and he's never come back. He can't be livin'.'

'Malcolm was lost, then, and came back. Magnus? When did he leave?'

'When it was still dark the day afore yesterday. We looked for him that day and yesterday, and this day, too, though we kenned he could no be livin', him near starvin' as he was.'

Willie stood still. Then he asked, 'You saw no sign of hunters that he could have gone with?'

'No, Willie, and he was lookin' for Malcolm; we had found meat.'

Willie was thinking. Magnus was gone for three days.

'If he were livin' he would be here,' continued Geordie.

Willie was silent for a time. Then he asked, 'Malcolm was lost?'

'Aye, out all the night, but we found him in the morning. Mansie missed him and went away north.'

'And you searched there?'

'There and along the river. But the plain's more trackless than the sea. No wind or tide to go by. There's no kennin' the way he went.'

'There's no kennin', as you say.' Willie thought for a minute. 'I've had little to eat. Will you heat up some of the meat for me and for yourselves. We must eat if it chokes us.' He hoped that the group would do something other than sit in sorrow.

By the light of the fire the two families and the two friends ate – first with difficulty, but the hunger that had lain within them for a week could not be ignored. Gradually they ate more naturally, and the stricken faces of the McPhersons relaxed; even the boy Malcolm appeared less miserable. Only Willie had to force the food down. Beyond the group and the log walls he had a vision of Magnus staggering on, not knowing where he was going, gradually growing weaker, and collapsing on the bare plain. Before he and Geordie went to their shack, he looked at Malcolm. This time, the boy had not been sacrificed. But Magnus? When Willie had told Magnus that Harold's death troubled him, Magnus had replied that it was Providence. But the fair brows had knitted.

Willie was up at daybreak. While the others slept in exhaustion, he lit a fire outside and started to cook some oatmeal he had brought from Fort Daer. Geordie awoke, and together they forced down the porridge with no salt and no milk. When they had finished, Willie said, 'Geordie, all last night I felt I was sitting beside the body of Magnus out on the prairie. Today I go to find it, or what's left of it.'

'You'll no find it, Willie, and even if you do, the wild beasts will have torn it to bits.'

'Yes, Geordie, but I must go.'

'It's no use, Willie; but since you must go, I'm comin'.'

'You must not, Geordie. We can't all leave these folks though the winter's over. Both men can walk little yet. You must stay.'

Geordie stood looking at the ground. 'First Mansie and now thee, Willie. I doubt if I'll see thee again.'

'I have the same feeling, Geordie, but go I must. 'Thoo're a boy o' good heart,' old Nellie said. 'Good-bye, Geordie boy.'

Willie turned away, his voice failing him, and set out to the plain with the long, slow stride of the Indian. Geordie stood like a stone, but Willie did not look back.

Late that day Willie found a torn, blood-stained bit of clothing, some bones bare of flesh, and a piece of scalp with fair hair on it. He sat down near, and remained all night long. In the early morning two hunters came. He

showed them the remains and asked them to report to
Miles Macdonell that Magnus Isbister had been lost on the
plains and had been devoured by wild beasts. They had
gone on their way, and Willie wandered westwards and
northwards.

Harold had died trying to save Magnus. Magnus had
died looking for Malcolm. He, Willie Fea, was not running
from anything any more, but going to meet what he felt
sure was his fate. Nothing called him back to Fort Daer
and Red River. His destiny now lay away to the Pigogomew where his parents had died, or at Cumberland lake
where he was born. The bickerings of the Hudson's Bay
officers with Miles Macdonell, the hostility of the Northwest
Company, the quarrels among the settlers, these had
nothing to do with him any more.

'Thoo'll hae to go back to thee mother's folk, boy.' Old
Nellie's words came back to him. The only help the
settlers had got was from Peguis and his Saulteaux. It was
as Tomison had said; his mother's people were a fine race.
Only half of him had been with his father's people. He
wandered on and on. The sun began to sink; he struggled
on towards it. It went out of sight, and the horizon seemed
to come to meet him. He plodded doggedly towards it,
growing weaker and more tired. He knew he could not go
much farther; yet when darkness fell he tried to reach it –
but it receded before him. He lifted each leg now with
difficulty, weak from hunger and fatigue. His bones would
lie scattered on the prairie with those of Magnus. The boy
Harold lay in his coffin in the kirkyard at Ardvik, his back
broken.

The stars came out, the Pole Star bright, and he turned
towards it. It seemed to grow dim, and a vision came to
him of Ayek and himself in a canoe, not at South Branch

House but at Cumberland Lake when they had first played together, and gone berry-picking in the hot days with their mothers, the mosquitoes hungry and biting. He felt he was wandering slowly between the bushes by the lake, and he was calling Ayek to come.

'Ayek! Ayek!' he called feebly as he stumbled on. The vision changed. He saw the moon dim in a dark blue sky low over the black silhouettes of the trees round Cumberland Lake. Voices came to him from a camp fire among the trees, mirage voices, calling him, Indian voices, the voices he had run from. He must go to them now. He struggled forward, and fell unconscious on his face, as he had done nineteen years earlier. Around him stretched the prairie full of darkness, stretching mile after mile west and north.

22

Epilogue January 17th, 1821

The early missionary was glad when his drivers arrived at the camp fire of a welcoming band of Indians. He was on his way to the Hudson's Bay forts west of Red River to marry Company men to their Indian wives, to baptise their children, and to speak with Indians on the way. Soon he was seated with them around the fire, and they feasted him on buffalo tongues. After the feast and after the pipe had been passed round, they invited him into their wigwams, and asked him if he had come to speak to the Indians about the Great Spirit. His driver acted as interpreter, so the missionary could not speak as he would have liked, the interpretations having to be kept simple.

Finding the tents cold, he went again to the fire, now low, and the Indians lay down for the night. One came to him, however, and sat beside him, a tall, lithe, eagle-featured man. The missionary was pleasantly surprised when he spoke to him in English.

'You come to speak to Indians of the Great Spirit?'

'Yes. I hope to speak to many of them, and to begin schools for the children. They will learn that which will mean their happiness.'

'About the Great Spirit?'

'Yes, and they will learn to write, and to read in God's book.'

'The book of the Great Spirit you call Bible?'

'Yes,' said the missionary in surprise.

'And you tell of the man nailed to the tree?'

The missionary was still more surprised. 'I did not think,' he murmured to himself, 'that any fur trader spoke about Him, only about skins and goods.'

The Indian heard. 'No white man,' he said. 'What you call half-breed.'

'He was not one of you. Where did he come from?'

'Not one of us. My band travel long way down there,' the Indian said, pointing south. 'In dark, moon like bow, hear man, no see. Man call again. Find him flat and done. Still breathe. Take him to thicket. Feed him. He grow strong. Tell us of man nailed to tree.'

'Is he here now?' asked the missionary eagerly.

'No, he go that way.' The Indian pointed north. 'Find mother's people. Cumberland Lake. Must find them, he say. We not see him more.'

The missionary thought for some time. Then he asked, 'How long ago was this?'

'Seven, eight moons of melting snows.'

'What was his name?'

'He no say. We call him man of blue mark.'

'The man of the blue mark? What blue mark?'

'On arm, blue mark.'

'Oh,' exclaimed the missionary, 'it would be a cross, like this,' he said, drawing a cross with a twig in the scorched earth near the fire.

The Indian looked at it. 'This,' he said, and drew a bow at the foot of the cross.

Author's Note

Like the press, history makes headlines of battle and murder and sudden death. This story occupies largely the time of the Napoleonic wars which raged over the world between 1794 and 1815, and also the time when bitter rivalry between fur companies erupted into savage violence and massacre. The story, however, is set at the fringes of the world struggle, and is one of humble people who had no heroic part to play, but whose lives were deeply affected. Men from the Orkney Islands had been going to North America in the service of the Hudson's Bay Company for almost a century when the story begins, and in 1811 the first of them went there as settlers to be followed by many more during the nineteenth century.

During the wars with France, some 3,000 men from Orkney served in the army or navy, the total population being only about 24,000. Quite a number of them were seized by press gangs and forced into the service. Naval press gangs stopped ships and took men on various occasions. Robert Louis Stevenson in *Records of a Family of Engineers* tells how his grandfather, the famous lighthouse builder, was appalled by the brutal attentions of the naval press gangs. The men in the lighthouse service, especially the sailors, had to wear medals and carry papers to protect themselves against the press gangs, and the zeal of volunteer patriots. They were particularly active in the Pentland

Firth, the stretch of sea separating the Orkneys from the mainland. On land, constables seized men who had been named by the local authority. Each parish was required to supply men, and, according to law, a list of the young men had to be drawn up and the names of the required number drawn by lot. What actually happened was that the landowners – the lairds – and the large farmers, took upon themselves to be the parish council, met in secret, and named certain men – never their own sons – whose names were handed to the local constables. The landholders had either to supply the men or be fined forty pounds for each man short. Pressing was used whenever the government called for more men. In 1805 after Trafalgar it eased, but started up again when casualties mounted in the Peninsular compaign.

At this time Canada was confined to Upper and Lower Canada along the St Lawrence. Lower Canada was largely French-Canadian. The earliest settlers of Upper Canada were people known as United Empire Loyalists. They were Englishmen who had settled in America, but who remained loyal to the British government during the War of Independence. At the end of the war they were regarded as traitors in the United States and fled to Canada in their thousands, where they took up land in what is now Ontario. Miles Macdonell, chosen by Lord Selkirk to be governor of the colony started at Red River, had been a captain in the Canadian Volunteers. When the unit was disbanded, he took up land in Upper Canada.

The vast tract around the rivers flowing into Hudson's Bay was known as Rupert's Land, and stretched from the Great Lakes west to the Rockies and north to the Barren Lands. The Hudson's Bay Company had been given a monopoly in this area in 1670 by Charles II. By 1800 the Company had posts scattered around Hudson's Bay and up the rivers almost to the Rockies. Its rival, the North-west Company, with headquarters in Montreal had posts from the St Lawrence, west to Lake Winnipeg, up the Saskatchewan to the Rockies and north to Great Slave Lake. The Northwest Company was so active that it almost put its rival out of business. Then, under the terms of Charles II's Hudson Bay Charter, Lord Selkirk was given leave to colonise a tract of land along the Red River. The Northwest saw in Lord Selkirk's proposed settlement a threat to its existence, and opposed it first by fair means and later by foul. The early settlers were victims of the struggle between the two great Companies for the Hudson's Bay Company did not want settlement either. In 1814 the settlement was broken up by the Northwesters, re-estab-lished, broken up again in 1816 when Governor Semple and twenty-one of his men were shot down by half-breeds of the Northwest; re-established by Selkirk himself and left with a body of disbanded Swiss soldiers to protect it from violence. Selkirk, however, having spent much of his fortune in launching settlements, and being prosecuted and given no justice in the courts of Upper Canada, died a worn-out man in Spain in 1820. By this time the North-west Company, having strained its finances in its efforts to win, was ready for union, and the two fur companies joined forces in 1821. They agreed to leave the existing settlement in peace, but discouraged further settlement for another fifty years. In 1867 the British North America Act was passed, and in 1869 Rupert's Land became part of the Dominion of Canada, its territories officially open to settlement.

The site of South Branch House, some twenty miles

south of Prince Albert, Saskatchewan, has a marker, part of the inscription reading:

> On June 24 1794, while the strength of the fort was reduced to four men by the spring brigade to York Factory, Gros Ventre Indians attacked and burned the fort. They savagely massacred the old women and children, and three of the Company's servants, Wm Fea, H Brough, and M Annal. The young women were carried into slavery. Only J C Van Driel escaped after hiding in an abandoned cellar for eight hours.

There was no such person as the boy William Fea; he is imagined.

John West, first Anglican priest to Red River took three Indian boys with him to his mission on his way down from Hudson's Bay in 1820. The boy christened Henry Budd, an orphan, proved able and in 1837 was made catechist and sent to The Pas, south of Cumberland House, to start a mission. Five years later, the Reverend John Smithurst visited The Pas and baptised thirty-eight adults, twenty-two school children, and twenty-seven infants in this sparsely inhabited Indian district. An Indian legend attributed Budd's success to the Indians having already heard the Christian story from a wonderful Indian named Kayanwas. The Epilogue is based on the legend.

3 9004 02607464 8

AFD1868

EDUCATION

DATE DUE

DATE DUE